LIGHT IN THE MOUNTAIN SKY

CALL OF THE ROCKIES ~ BOOK 3

MISTY M. BELLER

Misty M. Beller
BOOKS

For thy mercy is great unto the heavens,
and thy truth unto the clouds.

Psalm 57:10 (KJV)

CHAPTER 1

Meksem might have made the biggest blunder of her life.

She couldn't agonize over the decision now, though. Not as her mount's hooves pounded into the pressed snow of the game trail. The thundering of her friends' horses thudded hard behind her.

If she let her mind dwell on the birthright she'd just traded away, she would lose sight of the mission before them—to catch up with the Blackfoot war party who'd kidnapped her half-sister. No matter what, she had to free Telípe from her captors and bring the girl safely back.

Telípe's husband was said to have already started out after her, leading a small group to catch up to the kidnappers and free the captives. Yet he'd been ill for over thirty sleeps, not able to keep food down. He must be impossibly weak by now.

Their mother would be beside herself. And Telípe's father. Their mother's second husband had spent many years protecting and providing for his family, but now Meksem's turn had come. Though she and Telípe shared only the same mother, the girl was family—her responsibility.

This rescue she could do. She had to.

Besides, she had a whole band of new friends to help. Maybe even too many friends. Seven, aside from her. Along with their mounts and packhorses.

How could they ride fast and sneak up on the Blackfoot with so many? She'd become accustomed to traveling with groups of warriors, but in those cases, she'd only been responsible for herself and making sure *she* didn't slow or burden the others.

Now, she owned responsibility for leading all these. She'd started this mission. It was her sister they'd set out to free. What if she led them astray? What if she led them into a trap?

She'd worked hard through the years to sharpen her senses. To perfect her aim with the bow and hone her abilities as hunter and protector. Able to match or best any warrior she came up against.

But what if all her work wasn't enough? What if *she* wasn't enough?

She'd already made one mistake that almost cost a friend's life. What if the next one proved fatal?

Locking her jaw, she pressed the traitorous thoughts aside and focused her gaze on the dark line running across their path ahead. A small river, a good place to slow the horses and let them catch their breath.

As she neared the water, she raised her hand in the signal to walk and reined her mare down from a lope. Apash shook her head and blew out a long breath as she stretched her neck. Meksem patted the mare. *You're doing well, my friend.*

She and Apash had traveled great distances together, and the horse hadn't failed her yet. Always a match to any steed the other warriors rode.

Turning in her saddle to see the group stringing out behind

in the gray afternoon sun, her gaze landed on Adam first, riding right behind her. Sitting tall and comfortable on his brown gelding, he looked at perfect ease.

And his eyes. Those uncanny orange eyes always gripped her, stealing her breath and drawing her in. When she'd handed him the spotted gelding and said *Yours*, the joy that sparkled in those startling eyes had made it even harder to look away.

The moment she'd seen the animal, she'd known Adam would love him. The same glow lit both their expressions. And the horse's coloring...she'd never seen such perfect markings. Such striking contrast between the pure white background and the black perfectly-round circles. She'd seen other horses with an eye-catching coat, but the lean musculature and the excellent proportions—all of it came together in this animal to form a horse any chief would prize.

In fact, the chief she'd traded with had treasured the animal a great deal. Nothing but her most precious possession would make him give up the horse, even though he owned a full herd of others.

A burn crept up the back of her throat as an image of the jade-handled tomahawk slipped through her mind.

She forced the memory and the emotions away, jerking her gaze from Adam to scan the others behind him. Her nearest friend, Elan, rode beside Joel, who was both Elan's intended and Adam's brother. Then came the big man, Caleb, then French, the one from the north who spoke like the trappers who often wintered in their village.

And in the rear, the Blackfoot brave, Beaver Tail, with his woman, Susanna. Meksem's stomach churned at the sight of his warrior expression. She'd still not grown to be at ease around the man after spending so many days with this group. The Blackfoot were sworn enemies of both of her tribes—her mother's Nimiippu, who the whites called Nez Perce, and her father's Salish.

This Blackfoot brave hadn't seemed cruel and treacherous, except perhaps during their first meeting when he'd sprung upon her in the darkness of a cave. Even then, he'd not pressed his advantage, only forced her and Elan into daylight so they could all come to an understanding of each one's purpose.

But now... Now that they tracked a band of Blackfoot kidnappers, how could she be certain this man didn't plan to take them all captive as soon as they neared his people?

She couldn't be certain.

Which was why she would watch him. Her life, Elan's life, and even her sister's life might depend on her diligence.

Turning to the trail ahead, she adjusted her position in the saddle as her mare descended the bank to the river. The water flowed freely, but not too fast. From what she remembered, the animals would only be wet to their bellies, and the distance across wasn't more than four or five horse lengths.

An easy crossing.

Apash stepped into the freezing liquid without hesitation. The mare possessed the perfect combination of trust in Meksem's guidance, courage to face any obstacle, and savvy ability to overcome complications that sprung up.

Several steps into the water, the mare paused to adjust her balance against the steady flow. Meksem glanced back to check those behind her. Adam's riding horse had stepped into the water, but the new spotted gelding balked at the bank's edge, pulling hard on the tether rope Adam held.

He crooned to the stubborn animal, the shift of his elbow showing his steady tugs, but nothing swayed the spirited horse.

Caleb nudged his mount up behind the Palouse gelding, crowding it so the animal might choose the more spacious option of charging into the water.

The gelding jerked its head back, half-rearing as its eyes flashed panic.

"Ho there. Easy, boy." Adam's settling voice grew louder to gain the horse's attention.

The calming words didn't penetrate the thick-headed animal's fear. The horse jerked and spun, charging into Caleb's mount as it pulled hard to free itself from the tether tugging it toward the water.

Caleb's horse stumbled from the force of the spotted gelding's blow, staggering backward. Meanwhile, the panicked horse squealed and lunged sideways, away from Caleb and his mount, ready to dart around the pair and run far from the frightening water.

"Ho!" Adam's voice rose above the melee. He held the tether rope tight as he struggled to turn his mount and follow the terrified gelding out of the water.

But the spotted horse wasn't waiting. Catching sight of a clear retreat beside Caleb's horse, he charged through the opening, jerking Adam out of the saddle.

Why didn't he let go?

Adam landed in the water with a splash, on his knees and struggling to his feet as the panicked gelding tugged him hard.

When he cleared the river, Adam gathered himself against the pull of the rope and bit out a sharp, "Ho!" He used his entire body as leverage against the fleeing horse.

The crazed gelding slowed, spinning sideways and jigging its front feet as it stared with wide eyes at the river.

"Settle down." Adam's voice shifted back to its soothing tone, although this version had more backbone to it as he took a slow step toward the horse. He kept the rope tight, but the animal didn't try to retreat from him.

In truth, the animal didn't seem afraid of Adam at all, only the river it seemed to think would surge up to eat the horse alive.

"That's enough now." Adam still advanced toward the gelding, moving hand over hand along the tight tether line as he spoke in that same calm-yet-determined tone.

When he reached the animal and slid a hand up its face to rub a palm over the flat spot between its eyes, the gelding finally dropped its head with a long sigh, giving in to the magic this man seemed to wield with animals.

Adam kept one hand rubbing the spot between the horse's eyes, then used the other to stroke its neck, working his way over the crest until he had the horse in something like a hug. The animal looked more like a lap-dog now than the crazed beast of moments before.

Adam glanced up at Caleb. "You all right?"

Caleb nodded, his hands propped over the front of his saddle in a relaxed pose as he watched Adam. "Me an' this ol' girl don't break easy."

Then Adam turned his gaze to Meksem, apology in his eyes. "Sorry for the delay."

What could she say? He hadn't meant for his horse to respond so fiercely to the river water. And *she'd* been the one to bring the animal along in the first place. She'd traded her inheritance for the gelding, after all. How could she quibble about a short delay?

But they'd never catch up with the Blackfoot at this pace. And Adam was soaked from the knees down. In this frigid air, he'd freeze. Maybe even lose some toes.

He must have seen her looking, for he dropped his focus to his feet, and a frown furrowed lines in his brow.

Then he jerked his head up. "You all go on across. Caleb, do you mind taking my riding horse with you? I think this youngster will go fine if I walk him at the same time the rest of you cross."

An uneasy churning started in her middle. She glanced out at the center of the river. The water wouldn't come to his waist, as best she remembered, but he'd be soaked. When they first found Adam in the Kannah village, he'd been on the doorstep of death from sickness. His body had burned with so much fever, he'd not awakened at all the first few days. He couldn't risk sickness like that again.

They'd have to take time to dry his clothing and warm him after he waded through the river. In truth, his leggings were already so wet they'd have to be dried. Perhaps soaking them a second time wouldn't make a difference. Either way, they'd have to stop and build a fire when they reached the other side.

He met her gaze, and his chin came up as his eyes sparked determination. "I won't hold you up any more than I already have."

Not true, but they had no choice at this point.

She turned her mare back toward the opposite side of the river and started forward again. She tipped her head just enough to keep an eye on the happenings behind her. Caleb grabbed the reins of Adam's riding horse and started through the water.

Adam led the spotted horse alongside Joel's mount and stayed side-by-side as they approached the river. The gelding paused at the edge, the whites of its eyes flashing fear and its nostrils flaring.

But then it stepped forward at the same time Adam did. The first hoof sank into the water, then a hesitant second hoof as it brought its back legs forward. The horse paused for a breath, then jerked the first front hoof up and plunged it forward again.

Step by step, the animal progressed alongside Adam, smoothing out its movements as its confidence grew. She couldn't hear Adam's low voice, but his lips moved as he spoke to the animal. Twice, he reached over and laid a hand on the gelding's neck, encouraging. The man had a way with horses, no doubt.

She could imagine exactly how the spotted gelding felt with Adam by its side. As though it had finally met someone who saw through the bluster to the fear and mistakes underneath, and looked past even those to the true being at the core.

There were times Adam looked at her that way. As though he saw both the person she really was and the person she wanted to be. The only other human who'd ever seen that had been her father.

Maybe that was the reason she'd traded her most prized possession for this horse she knew Adam would love so much. If she could give him this joy, maybe the gift would be thanks enough for the way he made her feel—fully known, and not lacking.

Except...now, the gelding couldn't be bringing much joy. Frostbite surely, but not joy.

When she reached the opposite bank, she turned Apash toward nearby trees that would provide shelter for a warming fire, then slid to the ground and started pulling out supplies. If they could get him warm quickly enough, they might cover a bit more distance before nightfall. She planned to push as far past dark as the horses could manage, but she'd have to watch the people, too.

Especially Joel, with all his injuries. She'd already shot the man with a rifle—albeit, accidentally—and she couldn't strike the final blow by wearing him out in the saddle.

Meksem moved through the copse of trees to find bark dry enough to burn. They carried dry wood with them to use in the night's fire, but they needed that for their camp later. Anything she could find for fuel now would be helpful.

"No fire." Adam's words stopped her short as she bent to scoop up a branch lying atop the snow.

She straightened and turned to where he dragged himself and the now-calm gelding from the river. Water streamed down his buckskin leggings. His breath clouded in the frigid air, which would grow even frostier as night progressed.

They had no choice. He had to dry out and get warm.

But as she turned back to her wood gathering, he motioned again for her to stop. "Give me a minute, and I'll be ready to keep riding."

Frustration swept through her. A minute was much shorter than the time it would take to build a fire, but every delay twisted inside her. If they waited very long, they may as well camp in this place. Telípe's weak and sickly husband would find her before Meksem did. And how would he overpower the Blackfoot captors?

Telípe might be lost forever.

If the Blackfoot made it back to their own territory, the girl would be condemned to unspeakable horrors.

She locked her jaw to hold in her anger. But as her mind told her to build a fire before she wasted any more time, her gaze fixed on Adam as he pulled out the furs from his bedroll.

He bent down and unlaced his tall moccasins enough to slide them off, then rolled his leggings up above his knees—then even higher, as far up as the wet leather would go. White flesh glared out at her, darkened a little by the dusting of black hairs that showed even across the distance between him. She glanced away as a heat crept up her neck. She'd seen other warriors' legs and never taken notice. Why did Adam's affect her?

Then he covered the exposed area with a wolf skin, wrapping the pelt around and around before strapping it tight with a rawhide tie. The fur enclosed the full length of his leg, all the way down to cover his foot. Not a single piece of flesh peeked out.

As he worked on the other leg in the same way, the others in their group gathered around. Everyone had made it through the river, and if they could keep Adam from taking sick, it appeared none would be the worse for crossing.

If Adam stayed well.

He'd successfully removed the wet leather from contact with

his skin, and maybe the fur would keep his legs and feet warm. Maybe.

When he finished wrapping both legs, he scooped up his soaked moccasins and tied them to hang from his saddle. They'd freeze before they dried, but at least they weren't hurting anything.

He didn't even glance her way as he took up the tether for the troublesome gelding, then paused to give the horse a gentle rub between the eyes. The animal dropped its head at Adam's touch, lowering its eyelids as though the single stroke soothed away every fear. Adam's mouth moved as he spoke to the horse. He gave his riding horse a pat on the shoulder, adjusted the fur over one foot to fit it in the stirrup, then mounted in a single, fluid motion.

Finally, he turned to her with a nod. "Ready."

Sitting there atop the brown horse with the spotted one calm at his side, Adam looked as confident as any man ever could. Even the thick fur wrappings around his legs seemed natural.

She wanted to dislike him, truly she did. She was used to competing with men, not feeling any soft emotions. But when he looked at her with that gentle smile, the corners of his eyes crinkling in a way that made her feel as though he saw and knew and liked her anyway, she couldn't keep herself untouched by this man.

That fact had already proved her downfall. If she wasn't careful, much more would be lost.

Even more than the treasure she'd already given up.

CHAPTER 2

*A*dam fought to keep his teeth from chattering as they rode northward. The furs around his legs might have been able to keep him warm if he hadn't started off just shy of frostbite.

But he couldn't slow the group down to warm himself.

Meksem's desperation hung in the air, thick and tangible and working its way through his insides. She and her sister must be close friends. Like he and Joel were.

He could imagine how he'd feel if Joel had been kidnapped by their fiercest enemies. He wouldn't stop to sleep, or eat, or even breathe until he saved his brother. And Joel would do the same for him—in fact, he'd already done so when he and these other men traveled for months to find Adam among the Nez Perce.

So he couldn't slow Meksem down by voicing this aching chill.

His new spotted gelding tossed its head beside his leg, so he loosened the tether line enough to give the horse a little more freedom.

A temperament like this animal possessed would fight

against a tight rope. The challenge in gentling him would be in not squashing his personality, but instead, partnering with it. Making the two of them one. Uniting in body and spirit so they worked as a single being.

And he could do it.

Just as he'd done with Fritz, all those years ago. Joel had thought Adam would hate the Andalusian stallion after the animal stomped him so fiercely, almost taking his life. But as he lay in bed week after week recovering, a yearning had grown inside him to tame the animal. To win him over, developing a respect between them—a bond where they could work together.

Over the next year, he'd accomplished that feat, and Fritz had become a devoted friend, no longer a stallion to be feared.

Now, he would do the same with this Palouse horse. This animal was a treasure—one Meksem must have traded a great deal for. He still didn't understand why she'd given him this gift. But he'd do his best to thank her by helping bring her sister home.

Another horse rode up beside him, and Adam glanced at his brother. Fine lines creased the corners of Joel's eyes, attesting to the pain he must be fighting. Within the past fortnight, he'd suffered both a gunshot wound and an extended dunking in a half-frozen river.

Adam released a shaky breath. Maybe he should've insisted Joel stay back. The two of them could've waited another day, then tried to catch up with Meksem and these others. Would that have been enough to help Joel, though?

They never would have caught up though. Not with the pace Meksem set.

Still, he should have put his brother's needs before his own desire for adventure. Would he ever get better at that? He always seemed to see his faults in hindsight. After the consequences from his choices affected those he loved.

"Elan said we should reach their village sometime tomorrow morning." Joel's voice dragged with exhaustion.

Adam nodded. "Is that if we don't stop to rest the horses tonight, or if we do?"

He meant the statement half teasing, but part of him wondered if Meksem might push on all night if she were alone. In truth, part of him wondered if she would make them ride through the dark hours anyway.

Joel sighed, an action only loud enough for Adam to hear. "Not sure if I can handle riding much longer without a rest."

Adam slid another look at his brother. Joel had mastered the art of persevering wherever Adam dragged him. For him to speak up now, he must feel half dead. "Maybe you and I should stay a while in Elan's village. Let the others go on." The words soured on his tongue, but he wouldn't take them back.

If his brother needed to rest, Joel deserved for his best interest to come first for once. Adam set his jaw. He'd do whatever he had to for Joel. Even let the others continue the adventure without them.

Joel's shoulders straightened. "We'll keep going. As long as I can ride without slowing them down."

A sinking feeling worked its way through Adam's belly. Slowing the group down might be the least of their worries.

Actually finding Telípe and getting her away from the Blackfoot war party would be a far bigger challenge.

～

She had to stop, no matter how much fear drove her forward.

Meksem guided her mare into the shelter of the aspen grove and reined in. As much as she wanted to keep going, they'd been riding in the dark for quite a while, and the horses needed time to rest and eat. The people probably did too.

She motioned to a flat area. "We'll build a fire and sleep."

Elan translated her words into the white man's tongue.

Meksem should have spoken their language herself. Elan's translation used the same words she'd thought were right. But for some reason, Meksem couldn't bring herself to speak that tongue unless she had to.

They all set to work, each member of the group falling into the rhythm of setting up camp, as they'd done the last time they'd traveled through the mountains together.

Only Adam hadn't been with them then.

He focused his attention on helping with the horses, which didn't surprise her. In fact, he stayed longer with the animals than anyone else did, coming to the fire only when Joel called him to eat. Surely he was frozen through after his soaking earlier in the day, even with furs still wrapped around his legs.

He eased down on a log beside the warm blaze and smiled at Elan when she handed him his portion of baked camas root and roasted elk meat on a strip of bark. Something twinged in Meksem's chest at that smile aimed toward her friend. But he'd only offered the look as an expression of gratitude. The man must be hungry, as they all were.

Meksem shouldn't want a smile from him anyway. She'd never let herself be distracted by a man, and she couldn't let that happen on this mission either.

"Sorry I'm late." He leaned forward into the fire's warmth. "Thought I'd spend a few minutes getting to know my new gelding." This time he aimed his grin toward Meksem, his orange eyes shining in the light of the flickering blaze. "I like him. A lot. One of the finest animals I've ever seen."

His words soaked through her like a warm stew on a cold night. Soothing. Nurturing. They offered the balm she needed to heal the edge of loss from what she's given up to get the horse for him.

His grin turned gentle, as though he sensed her pain. How

could he see everything she worked so hard to hide? No one except her father had ever been able to see through her like that. And that had been so many years ago.

She looked away, and silence settled over the group as they ate, weariness hanging thick in the air. They were all wise to conserve their words…their energy.

As much as her own body craved sleep, the restlessness inside her might make it hard to doze off.

What was her half-sister doing on this dark night? Did her captors allow Telípe to sleep? Has she been given a fur covering to protect her from the frigid cold? What of warm food, or any food at all?

They had to get to her soon. Had to free her from her captors.

Meksem should have pushed longer this night instead of stopping when the moon reached the peak of the sky.

Quiet murmuring drifted from where Elan and Joel spoke in low tones. He seemed far more exhausted than the others, with face pale and cheeks drawn. In truth, he looked ill.

Would he be able to manage the journey? This first day had been easy over level ground. Sure, she'd kept them moving at a quick pace. But still…

She'd been a fool for allowing him to come. Not only because he would slow her down, but because a man could only handle so much before his body gave out.

She fought to keep from cringing at the memory of him lying on the snowy ground, blood spreading in a widening circle over his belly. Would she ever be able to put that accidental shot out of her mind?

She'd never apologized to him. Not a true apology anyway. Warriors didn't admit they'd done something wrong. Even when they'd not meant the act at all. But she needed to speak to him of the incident.

To explain. To tell how much she regretted what happened.

Raising the topic might help them both. Or maybe she was only being selfish once more.

~

"*E*asy, boy. Time to hit the trail again." Adam stroked the spotted gelding's neck with one hand while the animal nuzzled his other palm. "We need to give you a name, don't we?" He'd have to ponder later, for he had no time to dwell on it now. "Let's get moving."

He untied the gelding's rope, then mounted his riding horse. He'd planned to try a packsaddle on the young horse this morning, but Meksem had awakened them before dawn with an impatient, *We ride now.* The intensity marking her strong features communicated her impatience clearly.

When they'd all mounted, even before they gathered in the open area beside the trees, Meksem turned her mare northward. He nudged his riding horse into step behind hers. Maybe he could say something to ease her strain.

"Any icy rivers to cross today?" he called ahead, keeping his tone light.

"Maybe." She turned her head just enough for the word to drift back to him, but not enough for him to see if her stern expression softened.

At least she'd spoken. In English too, which she didn't use often.

"Elan said we'll reach your village this morning."

A nod offered her only answer.

"Do we need to stop there for supplies?" They'd traded for as much as they could at the village they'd left yesterday, but Meksem knew the land they'd be traveling on this journey. She would know best what they were lacking, if anything.

She turned her gaze to the mountains on their right, her look distant.

He held his tongue. She would answer when she wanted to, and they had several hours to make the decision.

At last she spoke, turning her head even more to the side so he could hear. He nudged his mount forward to ride alongside her.

"There is nothing we need enough to stop." Her words were halting, but she spoke English. Albeit with a strong accent. She had a beautiful voice, strong but melodic. Those two qualities didn't seem to go together, but with Meksem the combination seemed natural. A contrast—just like the woman herself.

Her brow still lowered, as though she wanted to say more but didn't know how.

He waited. Maybe if he knew her tongue, she would speak more to him. But perhaps language wasn't the reason for her silence. She seemed quiet by nature.

"I think Joel should stay in our village." She didn't look at him, just kept her focus ahead.

Adam's chest tightened. So he'd not been the only one thinking such. But that would mean Adam would need to stay too.

So be it. The time had come for him to stop being so selfish.

He nodded, holding in his sigh. "You're probably right."

~

Tension lingered in the air as Meksem halted her horse and turned to face the others. Exhaustion dragged at Joel's expression, slumping his shoulders. He must realize he couldn't keep up the pace she needed to travel.

Meksem shifted her gaze to her long-time friend. Instead of the stubborn look she'd expected, Elan's features curved into a knowing almost-smile. What scheme did she have planned? They'd been friends long enough for Meksem to recognize the confident expression Elan wore when she plotted something.

She turned her focus back to Joel. "Our village is ahead. The journey will be too much for everyone to go. Some should stay." She used her own tongue, then looked to Elan to translate.

She listened closely to Elan's interpretation to make sure her friend didn't change the meaning. As much as she trusted Elan, her friend might not even realize a shift in words that would give Joel the wrong idea about her intent.

But Elan spoke true. As she finished the translation, Joel's chin rose, and his shoulders straightened. He slid his gaze from Elan to his brother.

Meksem had determined not to look at Adam. He would want to stay with his brother—the blood tie held strong between them, as it should be. But she couldn't bear to watch him choose to leave her.

Elan had barely finished translating when she turned to Meksem. "I will stay with Joel. My mother and father will want to know him." The glance she sent sideways at her intended spoke more than her words did.

Joel studied her, his brow lowered as though he warred within himself. His focus shifted from Elan to Adam, then moved one by one to each person in the group.

At last, he looked at the ground as his throat worked. He dipped his chin in a single nod. "All right." He inhaled a breath and turned to Elan with another nod. "We stay. We meet your parents." A hint of a grin touched his mouth. "It's time."

Elan's demeanor relaxed, and she looked to Adam. "You go with Meksem." Then she sent Meksem a smile, as though pleased with the way she'd worked things.

The knot in Meksem's chest didn't loosen. She should be pleased with the outcome. Joel would be safe here where he could rest and recover. Elan too. This seemed the right choice for them.

But Adam… She'd thought he would stay with his brother, and now the shift had her mind off-kilter. Why did she hesitate for him to accompany her? Just moments before she'd been sad that he would be leaving her.

Was it the way he affected her? Maybe. She couldn't allow herself to be distracted on this journey. The stakes were too high. Her sister's life depended on them reaching her in time. Then on their ability to free her.

No matter what, Meksem would have to guard her heart. She'd have to force away all distractions.

Especially the handsome one named Adam Vargas.

CHAPTER 3

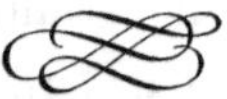

"*D*o you want me to stay?" Adam's gut twisted as he stood beside Joel in the Nez Perce camp, awaiting his brother's response.

Joel didn't even pause as he shook his head. "Go." Then his mouth tipped in a half grin. "Meksem will be there to take care of you. The others too."

Adam couldn't help a chuckle. "Right."

Joel had long ago appointed himself as his brother's protector. No matter that Adam was the elder. After the family's Andalusian stallion Fritz nearly stomped the life out of him, Joel had stayed by Adam's bedside for weeks, entertaining him while he recovered. They'd been best friends before that, but something in Joel had changed during that time. As though he'd determined never to let death near Adam's door again.

Adam had never minded Joel's overprotectiveness. In truth, he would have been lost without his brother by his side these past years, through every adventure they'd experienced together. Not just the journey from Spain, but so many experiences before that. And twice as many since.

But now the time had come for Joel to live his own life. To meet his soon-to-be parents-in-law.

Adam had to let him go.

Joel reached out a hand in farewell, and Adam gripped it, then pulled him into a hug.

"I'll come back." Emotion clogged his voice, turning it husky. "Don't worry about me." He swallowed down the burn and cleared his throat as he pulled away. He had to blink to clear his vision. "I'd like to say 'don't get married until I return,' but I suppose that's not fair to you." He tightened his grip on his brother's hand and met Joel's gaze. "You have my blessing."

Joel nodded, squinting. Probably against the moisture in his own eyes.

Adam gave Joel's hand a final squeeze and grabbed his shoulder with his other. Then he turned away. "Meksem's itching to ride out. I need to go."

He strode to where the others waited, took his mount's reins from Caleb, then swung up into his saddle.

When he looked back for a final farewell, Joel stood next to Elan, tucking her close to his side. Two figures standing alone, yet together. They would have each other now.

After a final wave, Adam faced the trail ahead and nudged his mount faster. They had a job to do, and he could no longer be a hindrance. It was time he take the lead.

They rode at a canter where the ground would allow it, slowing to a walk over the rockiest stretches. Meksem had them dismount once to lead the horses, allowing the animals to catch their breath. But then they were back in the saddle, riding at a steady lope.

As dusk turned to twilight, they reached the first of the mountains. The foothills, Meksem called them. She slowed the group to a walk, and Adam reined his mount up beside hers. "Will we ride through the village where your sister lived?"

She shook her head. "Camp is that way." She pointed to the

left, back toward the rolling prairie land. "We ride straight to Blackfoot country." She motioned at the mountains in front of them.

"Any idea how far ahead the kidnappers are?"

She squinted, peering into the distance. Calculating, maybe. Although, she'd probably been turning days and riding times over and over in her mind until she knew almost to the minute, so maybe she was only deciding how much to tell him.

"One day and a half. Two days. Hard to tell." She accompanied the words with a shrug.

Two days. How fast would the war party be moving? Surely having the captives would slow them down. "Should we ride through the night?" Could the horses handle it? Maybe if they alternated riding their usual mounts with the packhorses.

He glanced sideways at her spotted mare. "Wish we all had Palouse horses like yours. She doesn't look tired at all."

Meksem's impassive warrior face softened as she reached down to pat her horse's neck. "She can go through night." She glanced at his mount, then behind them at the others. The smooth line of her brow furrowed. "Maybe if we don't always ride. Walk some."

He nodded. "We won't stop to camp then." If the horses showed signs of wearing out, he could call a halt. But for now, they had to keep moving.

A movement ahead jerked him to attention, and he squinted to see in the fading light. Riders rounded a bend in the trail. Indians, but he couldn't tell which tribe they were from.

Four of them. About forty strides ahead.

He glanced sideways at Meksem. She didn't look worried, only held her head high, her back rigid in the warrior stance. She always rode with her bow and quiver of arrows strapped on her back where they would be easy to reach, and she didn't grab them now.

He turned his focus back to the approaching strangers. All

men, from what he could see. "Do you know them?" He kept his voice low enough that his words wouldn't carry to the group riding toward them.

"Salish. Hunting party." She spoke in the same quiet tone.

Good.

When they met the oncoming riders, the brave in the lead signed a friendly greeting. His gaze scanned their party, probably not sure what to think about such a varied collection of people.

Meksem exchanged a quick conversation with the man—mostly pleasantries, from the few words Adam could pick out. Then her tone grew more intense, her sentences chopped, her words almost angry. She must be asking about the Blackfoot kidnappers.

The other man shook his head as he rattled off an answer. His expression looked regretful. Maybe he didn't have any helpful information.

Meksem only nodded in response, then bit out a farewell.

Their group waited as the hunting party passed, then Meksem pushed her mare forward. She didn't act as though she planned to explain the conversation. In truth, she seemed so determined—so driven—he almost hesitated to ask her anything.

But if they were to be successful in this mission, their group would need to work together as a team. As capable as Meksem might be, using their collective ideas and experiences would surely be better than relying on her plans alone.

When the trail widened enough for him to ride alongside her, Adam nudged his horse forward. "Did they have news? Anything of the Blackfoot party or the rescue group that went out from your sister's village?"

Meksem shook her head. "They are not from same Salish camp. Have heard of the attack but nothing more."

He couldn't help but notice how much more English she'd

been speaking that afternoon. Was it because he sought her out to ask questions? Mayhap she knew the words but hadn't felt comfortable using them unless prompted.

"So you learned nothing new from them?"

The strong line of her jaw hardened, and she didn't answer right away.

Finally, she spoke. "I learned my sister is with child."

The words swirled through Adam's mind, taking a moment to form into a coherent thought.

With child? And she'd been kidnapped, possibly beaten and abused, maybe starved? What would that do to the baby? How much more danger did that add to her own chances?

Intense urgency surged through him, and he had to breathe hard to keep from kicking his mount into a run.

"We have to find them." His voice came out low. Hard.

Meksem nodded, and the determined set of her profile made her agreement clear. No matter what the journey required, they had to free Telípe.

They had no time to waste.

~

Darkness hung thick around Meksem as she strained to see the trail ahead. Only a tiny sliver of moonlight peered through the cloud cover, and, with the dense forest they rode through, she could barely make out her hand in front of her.

Surely the night would end soon. Maybe even now, the great sun rose on the other side of the mountains. But the scrawny branches growing up on either side of them, closing over top of them, smothered out the light. Suffocating her with the weight of her fear.

Telípe carried a child.

Meksem's muscles tightened. Her own worry must be

nothing to what weighed on her sister. She could imagine the scene now, Telípe struggling to keep up with the others, beaten and kicked because of the weariness that assaulted all women growing a new life within them. If the warriors struck her belly, what could Telípe do to protect her innocent babe? She would clutch her middle and curl around herself. But another blow might bring blood. So much blood.

The child inside her would die. Telípe might bleed to death right there, curled in the snow.

At the hands of the Blackfoot dogs.

"Look." Susanna's voice drifted from behind her, tugging her from the awful vision.

Meksem glanced back to see where the woman pointed. Through the trees, a faint glow edged along the top of the mountain.

Sunrise at last. Little by little, light crept through the mountain sky. The sight lifted a little of the weight from her chest. A new day meant another chance to close the distance between them and the sister who needed her so desperately.

As if one good thing brought on another, the woods around them thinned, and another few strides brought them into the open. Her mare clambered onto a rocky section as the path wound higher. Many animals had traveled this trail, likely goats and sheep with horns bigger than their heads. Antelope and elk, and surely mountain lions prowling for their next meal.

"Should we stop to eat a bite?" Susanna's voice sounded thin with the weariness that came from riding through the night. A few minutes to rest might be good for them all, both the people and the horses. Maybe she should have insisted Susanna stay at the village with Elan, but then Susanna's Blackfoot husband would have stayed as well.

Would that have been best? Indecision swirled in Meksem's belly, as it always did when she thought of the man. Beaver Tail had shown no signs of unfriendliness these past weeks she'd ridden with the group. But she still couldn't imagine a *good* Blackfoot.

That tribe had always been the enemy. With their guns from the white man, they brought grief and heartache whenever they crossed the mountains to the land of the Nimiipuu and Salish.

Even if Beaver Tail meant no harm to her and the other Salish captives, would he really fight against his own brethren?

On the other hand, if he could be persuaded to help, he should be able to tell much about the mountains they would be traveling through soon. And too, he would have great insight into the fighting ways of his tribe.

His help might mean the difference between freeing Telípe or losing her forever to her captors. Or worse yet—death.

Meksem halted her mare at a wide spot in the path. A flat boulder rested beside them—a good spot to sit once they wiped the snow away.

One glance at Susanna huddled in her fur coat sent a twist of regret through Meksem. White people had a harder time in the cold than those of her tribe. Maybe it wasn't too late to send Susanna back.

Maybe all of these people should return to the plains.

She didn't let herself look at Adam. Being without his distracting presence would help her focus.

Susanna and French propped themselves on the rock, but the others stood as they ate a simple meal of cold meat.

Meksem straightened to draw their attention. She met Susanna's gaze as she spoke. "I should not have brought you this far." She turned her focus on Beaver Tail. "You must go back to Elan's village." Then to French and Caleb. "The cold is too much for white men. Harder for those not from our mountains. I would not have your deaths on my hands."

Susanna was already shaking her head. She looked as though she would speak, but Caleb beat her to it.

"No, ma'am. We're all in this together. We crossed these

mountains once, we know what we're up against. We'll not leave you." His weary face pulled into a tired half-grin. "You're one of us now."

His words sent a warmth through her, nearly stealing the strength from her exhausted limbs. *You're one of us now.* How could he say that? They'd only known her the length of a single moon. They only saw what she allowed them to see. The face of a warrior.

She shook her head. "I need to go alone. It's best for all of us."

Beside her, she sensed Adam preparing to speak. Could hear the intake of his breath, and she braced herself.

"We're going together, Meksem. We'll be stronger—better— together. Speak no more of it."

Just like a pompous warrior, telling her the way things would be. What she could say and do—and what she couldn't.

But when he added a gentle "please," the tension loosened in her chest. Giving in would be so easy.

Yet, did she really have to make the decision? These people could do as they wished. They could tag along if they wanted to, but she didn't have to let them slow her down.

She would set her own pace. Charge ahead as she needed to. If they chose to keep up, so be it.

CHAPTER 4

A fog had settled in Adam's mind hours before, and the brightness of the winter sun on the snow crystals only made the sensation worse as they rode through the day.

Not only did the fierce glare blind him, his sleep-deprived mind made him feel as if he were seeing the world around him from a distance. As though he sat perched in the sky, watching himself ride second in line behind Beaver Tail as they wound in a switch-back pattern up the side of the mountain.

When light had fully settled that morning, Beaver Tail had recognized the area they were traveling, although he didn't give details of when or why he'd been on the western side of the mountains. Perhaps his silence was wise, given the Blackfoot's reputation for raiding parties.

Meksem had allowed Beaver Tail to take the lead without complaint. Did she feel as numb from lack of sleep as Adam did? She'd dropped to the back of their line, taking up Beaver Tail's former position. Rear guard. Protecting their flank.

If Adam weren't so exhausted, he might smile at the thought. Meksem—always the fierce warrior, ever protecting, no matter what the cost to herself.

But he didn't like the woman being so far back where he couldn't keep an eye on her. What if she fell asleep and toppled from her horse? Who would see and help her?

Meksem could be fierce and strong all she wanted, but someone needed to watch over her.

He wanted to be the one to watch over her. The realization both surprised him and weighed heavily in his heart. Could he protect her on such a dangerous mission? He slid a glance over his shoulder to take in the rest of the party. Susanna rode just behind him. She seemed to have appointed herself the encourager in the group, but even she didn't offer a cheerful smile just now.

Behind Susanna, French's head bobbed in rhythm with his horse's stride, probably half asleep, knowing French. They'd often joked of his ability to doze and ride. In the past, anyway.

Next came Caleb, who nodded a solemn greeting Adam's way.

Finally, bringing up the rear, Meksem sat straight as an arrow, not looking the least bit dazed from lack of sleep. How did she possess such strength?

He'd best turn around and tend to business at hand. As Adam twisted forward to the trail ahead, the Palouse gelding at his right jerked back, head raised, eyes wide. Before Adam could react, the animal slammed toward him, thrusting its body into his leg.

He barely had the presence of mind to jerk on the tether strap as his muddled thoughts scrambled to catch up with what was happening. The horse had been so calm after these many hours on the trail. Had a wild animal bitten it? Or maybe the gelding heard a sound none of the others had.

The horse loosed a high-pitched scream as it surged forward.

"Hey!" Adam yanked hard on the rope. His mount side-stepped away from the frantic gelding, and Adam pulled on his reins. The action only succeeded in turning his riding horse to face the panicked gelding.

"Let him go!" Susanna's cry pierced his churning thoughts.

He couldn't release the spotted horse. Not this prized animal, the finest Palouse gelding he'd ever seen. This special gift from Meksem.

Even as he tightened his grip on the rope, the young gelding reared, kicking out at Adam's mount as though Satan himself were shooting fiery arrows at it.

"Ho, boy." Adam's mind finally pushed away the remnants of sleep-deprived fog. He jumped down so he could better settle the spotted gelding. "Easy there."

The horse spun and lurched backward, almost pulling the rope from Adam's grip. Desperation widened its eyes and flared its nostrils as the animal fought to flee some danger only it could see.

"Steady." Adam kept his voice singsong and moved forward to loosen the tether line. "Settle now."

The animal backed away, pulling the rope tight again. But its head lowered a little, some of the fear fading.

Adam kept crooning to the horse, moving forward so it didn't feel threatened by the tight line. One step at a time, he closed the distance between them, keeping just enough pressure to stop the animal from moving backward. What in the great ball of sunlight had caused the animal to lose its wits?

Finally he reached the horse and raised a hand to rub the gelding's forehead. The animal dropped its head with a deep sigh.

"Thatta boy."

The horse leaned into his hand as if thankful for someone brave enough to slay whatever dragon had frightened it.

As strong and powerful as this gelding seemed, he really was simply an overgrown colt. Still a youngster trying to make sense of the frightening world around him. These snow-covered mountains were enough to strike fear in any creature—man or animal.

After a few minutes of calming the gelding, Adam glanced at the others sitting atop their mounts, watching him. "I think we're ready."

Beaver Tail shook his head. "That horse doesn't always think with his mind."

If Adam wasn't so tired, he might've smiled at the words. "He's still a youngster."

After giving the gelding a final pat on its neck, Adam turned to lead it back to his riding horse. The older animal stood waiting patiently, a good example for the colt.

He'd only taken one step when an ear-splitting crack exploded in the distance.

The spotted horse leapt forward, slamming into Adam's back. The blow knocked him down, and the force kept charging into him. The animal's chest rammed him into the snow. Something hard—maybe a hoof or a knee—slammed into Adam's backside.

A scream ripped the air, and voices clamored around him.

Icy cold tingled over his face and neck as pain surged up his back. Beside him, the spotted gelding went down to its knees, the rope pulling free from Adam's hand as the horse landed hard on its side. The animal rolled down the steep slope. Adam scrambled for the rope, anything to stop his priceless treasure from pitching down the mountainside.

After a single roll, the horse stopped itself, bracing its feet in the snow.

"Adam, get up!" French was at his side, grabbing for his arm. "Avalanche. The top of the mountain is breaking loose."

A new fear pulsed through Adam's chest, and he struggled to his feet. A glance up the slope proved French's words to be true.

Another loud crack echoed across the mountainside, but not as violent as the first one. A puffy white cloud billowed from the mountain's peak as parts of the solid sections of snow slid downward. If the icy layers stayed on the route the avalanche seemed to be sliding, the mass would plummet onto the trail just in front of them.

Their group couldn't chance staying in its path. Any twist of the rock face could change the course of the disaster.

"Up, boy." He pulled hard on the gelding's rope.

The horse scrambled to its feet, stumbled once, then righted itself.

"I've got your riding horse." French grabbed up the older gelding's reins along with his own and started tugging the horses back the way they'd come.

Adam pulled the spotted gelding forward. "Come on."

Beaver Tail moved his mount in behind the gelding, herding him onward.

For once, the spotted gelding walked forward obediently. Adam's backside throbbed, but he ignored the pain, tugging the horse into a trot. He had to march high to clear the snow, which rose up to his knees in some places.

The roaring swoosh of the avalanche grew louder, and he dared a glance up the mountain. The sliding snow had widened into a mighty wave, spreading and gaining momentum as it went.

They had to get away from the slide's path. The way the avalanche was growing, the outer edges would sweep over them. He pushed himself harder, lunging through the snow with the nervous gelding trotting beside him, jerking sideways at the tether rope. Ahead, the others were pushing their horses as fast as they could struggle through the icy covering on the uneven trail. One horse and rider had moved out of the line, and slowed to look back at them.

Meksem.

"Go!" He waved her onward. Why would she put herself in danger to wait for them?

She didn't obey. But he didn't have the energy to argue with her. He focused all his efforts on plowing forward.

Exhaustion dragged at him, but another glance upward showed the coming wave had already covered over half the distance to reach them. With each second, the mass seemed to stretch wider, as if determined to curl its snowy fingers over them.

He'd never been in an avalanche, not even in the snow-covered peaks of his homeland. But he'd heard stories of unsuspecting hikers covered by sudden snow slides, suffocating in their snowy graves.

Meksem sat atop her horse, a lone figure. The others had pushed hard to get out of the way. Why didn't she go with them? Only Beaver Tail kept his mount and packhorse behind Adam, herding the spotted gelding forward.

Adam motioned his friend around. "Go on. Get out of the way." With the roar of the snow growing louder, Beaver might not have even heard him.

Meksem rode toward him, holding out a hand. When he reached her, she yelled above the noise, "Ride behind me."

She had room on the back of her saddle, and she wasn't encumbered by a packhorse. Maybe his spotted gelding would trot along beside them. The animal seemed too afraid to do anything but obey.

Adam took hold of her arm as she gripped his, then put his foot atop her stirrup and swung up behind her. He'd barely landed behind the saddle when she started her horse at a walk to let the gelding settle in beside them. The animal moved forward willingly, even when she pushed into a trot. Beaver riding herd behind them probably helped nudge the gelding along.

They covered the distance three times faster than he would have trudging on foot through the deepening snow. Within moments, they reached the rest of the group, which had stopped beside a cluster of pines to wait for them.

Adam glanced up the mountain again. The snow would reach their level in seconds, but only a fog-like cloud extended as wide as they were. Did that cloud contain more than a dusting of swirling snow? Maybe it hid a thick mass of ice and stone. Better not to chance danger.

"Let's go farther." He waved them forward. Even now, he could feel the icy crystals tingling around his neck. Maybe the sensation was only leftover snow from when he'd fallen face-first on the ground, but his pounding pulse told him they still weren't safe.

Caleb led them onward, and Adam focused on staying calm so the nervous horse beside him didn't feed off his fear.

As the snow whooshed behind them, even Meksem's mare began to tremble beneath him. If she darted forward, he'd be pulled backward by the gelding's lead rope. He wrapped a hand around Meksem's waist to hold himself secure.

The moment his arm closed around her, his body honed in on the sensation of being so near her. Of touching her.

These were the last thoughts that should be swirling through his mind when danger pushed from every direction, but the lithe woman in his grasp filled his senses and stole his focus.

Meksem kept her horse moving, and, finally, the endless sounds of sliding snow behind them eased to a low murmur. When silence settled, Caleb signaled for them to halt.

The big man turned his mount to face the group and wiped a sleeve across his brow. "Whew. Thought we'd all seen our last there for a minute."

Adam inhaled a long breath, then released it in a slow stream. He was still achingly aware of his hand around Meksem's waist, so he pulled back a little, moving his palm to her side. A place where he could still grab hold if he needed to, but not quite so intimate. Yet, he could still feel every movement she made.

Meksem glanced back, but not at him. He twisted to follow her gaze to the loose snow covering the trail as high as the horses' backs.

"We cannot ride through there." Her breath fanned his face as she spoke.

Intoxicating. His belly churned, and he struggled to keep from falling into the haze of her nearness. Struggled to pull his mind onto her words and what he should do about them.

The snow would be too soft for them to follow the trail they'd been traveling. The avalanche had obliterated the icy crust the horses needed in order to walk on top of the snow. Even if the animals could struggle through that mass, the effort would wear them out, especially after riding all night with only limited rests.

He glanced at Beaver Tail. "Is there another way around?"

Grooves etched in his friend's brow as he gazed up at the mountain, then followed its line to the left and right. His focus stalled somewhere up high, maybe on the right side of the peak.

"I need to scout. See what's still possible." He glanced back at his wife, Susanna. "Rest until I return."

Under Adam's hand, Meksem tensed. "I ride too. With both of us, we find the best way."

Beaver Tail's face didn't show any sign of his thoughts. "One of us should stay and help with the horses. I know of another path, I only need to make sure it's not covered with too much snow."

Surely Meksem would see the wisdom in conserving their strength. Maybe if Adam started the process to get them settled in a small camp, she would consent to rest with them.

He leaned sideways to dismount, and a stab of pain shot through his right hip. He had to lock his jaw against a grunt as he swung his leg high enough to clear Meksem's packs. When his feet landed on solid ground, another piercing ache shot through him. Back when the gelding nearly ran over him, the animal must have landed hard on his right buttock. Bruises had surely already formed, but there was no way he would mention the pain.

He'd have to push through. Weakness and injury would only slow them down, and that he couldn't allow.

CHAPTER 5

The chance to sit and rest and fill his belly with food—even cold food—was exactly what Adam needed. If he weren't half frozen, the urge to sleep might be more than he could resist. At least his fur coat kept the snow from penetrating to his skin as he sat on the mountainside, and the cold from the ice under him numbed the pain in his hip.

"You've an awful lot more patience with that horse than I would, Vargas." French reclined in the snow nearby, arms crossed and a twig stuck in the corner of his mouth. The twist of his lips showed he meant the words in jest. Probably.

Adam's gaze drifted to the spotted gelding. The horse stood quietly, head lowered in a doze. Against the background of snow, its black spots stood out in bold contrast, illuminating the strength of its rippling muscles. One of the finest specimens of horse he'd ever seen. And he'd sensed something before the avalanche had happened. Maybe he possessed an uncanny intuition.

"He just needs a bit more time to learn to trust." After many hours together, the gelding would know he didn't need to startle at every danger. He'd be willing to work in tandem with Adam until they were protecting each other, trusting each other. Drawing strength from each other.

"What do you call him?" Susanna was sitting by the food pack, rolling the baked camas root back into its leather wrapping.

"Haven't decided yet."

Susanna squinted at the animal "You want something to do with his spots? Maybe Leopard? Or simply Spot."

Adam couldn't help wrinkling his nose. "Not quite right."

Her face turned thoughtful. "Maybe something to do with his temperament. How about Spirit, or Spooky."

He raised his brows. "I think not."

"You should give him a French name." French leaned on one elbow and pulled the twig from his mouth. "Something like Pointé or Dynamique. I had a yellow horse one time named Rafele. Smartest animal I've ever seen. Could untie any rope. If I left him tied to a hitching rail, he'd free himself, then walk down and set all the other horses loose."

"Oh yeah?" Caleb's voice held enough skepticism to prove he didn't buy the story any more than Adam did.

French pressed his hand to his heart. "As sure as I'm sitting here. I tried my best to break him of the trick. Even when I hobbled him, he just dropped his head down and untied the knots."

"So what did you do? Did you ever stop him?" They usually humored French when he told his wild stories, but Caleb sounded as if he half believed this one. Or at least he wanted to hear more.

The corners of French's mouth twitched. "He found a lady horse he liked and gave up his troublesome ways."

Caleb wrinkled his nose. "That's not a bit true."

French's eyes widened as if he couldn't believe Caleb would say such a thing. "Upon my honor as a Frenchman, every word is fact."

Caleb snorted, and Adam couldn't help the urge to do the same. Either that or grin.

"I saw how much he liked the mare, so I traded for her and used her as a packhorse. From then on, he never untied another knot. I figured he had no more reasons to run off."

A chuckle slipped from Caleb, and he shook his head. "You're too much some days, Frenchy."

"Always my aim." He sent a wink Susanna's direction.

A shuffling noise sounded from the mountain above them, and Adam jerked his gaze to the place. Sometimes one avalanche could set off others.

But the dark figure making his way down the slope eased the knot in Adam's chest. The incline was so steep, Beaver Tail had to move his horse in a slow switchback pattern as he descended.

Long painful moments passed as he worked his way toward them, and, by the time he reined his gelding to a stop, tension had coiled through Adam's muscles once again. The man's face gave no sign as to whether he bore good news or not.

They were all standing by the time he slipped from his mount. "We can go that way. The path is steep and rocky, but we should be able to manage if we move slowly."

Meksem stood just behind Adam, so he couldn't see her response to the words. But he could feel her. Could sense the hope that grew a little more with each statement, like a swimmer rising from the water and taking in her first breaths of air. But, with the final word *slowly*, she was plunged back under the surface, sealing off her ability to breathe. They couldn't move slowly. Every hour mattered.

Adam turned her way, locking his gaze with hers. Willing her to feel the truth in his words. "This is good. At least there's a way."

Her mouth formed a grim line as she nodded. "We ride now."

The horses seemed refreshed by their short break, a good thing because the steep ascent strained both their muscles and their breathing. The old bay gelding he rode did its best to keep up, but, by the time they stopped for another rest midway up the mountain, the animal's sides heaved as it gulped deep breaths of icy air.

Adam dismounted and stroked the horse's neck. "You all right, boy?" His new Palouse gelding barely seemed winded. It hadn't been carrying a rider and was probably at least fifteen years younger, but the difference in the two mounts still showed clearly. Too bad he couldn't ride the spotted horse.

He lifted his gaze to the others, and he saw Meksem watching him. He patted the bay's neck. "The incline is hard for him. I think I need to walk the rest of the way up."

A line pressed into her brow, and she gazed up the slope. The part remaining looked steeper and rockier than what they'd covered so far.

"Our trail over the top is just to the right of that boulder." Beaver Tail pointed toward one side of the crest.

"I should probably walk too." Caleb rubbed his hand over his mare's neck. "I'm a big fella for this gal to hoist."

Meksem nodded, and it might have been his imagination, but her shoulders seemed to dip a little. Walking would slow them down, but if one of the horses took sick from working so hard at the higher elevations, they'd be in worse trouble.

The next hours crawled by. Between the pain in his back-side that pressed all the way up to his shoulders and the frequent falls that scraped his knees against the icy rocks, his entire body screamed. He'd be a mix of black and blue by morning.

At least none of the horses slipped on the rocks, a fact that might just be a miracle.

And perhaps God did have something to do with the animals' safety, because behind him, he could hear Caleb praying more often than not. The man spoke as though God were right there with him, climbing over rocks and slipping in the snow. Wet, ragged, exhausted—and still with the power to see them safely to the other side of this mountain.

Where had Caleb formed such a friendly view of the Almighty?

Adam had always done what his parents and priests expected of him when it came to religion, but God seemed a distant Being. A Ruler settled on His throne, watching the actions of people with a critical eye. Only the rites and sacraments and prayers of the pious made Him look with favor on those who sought His attention.

Yet Caleb spoke as though he knew the Almighty well. Better even than he knew French or Beaver Tail, and these three men had traveled together at least two years now. The thought seemed impossible.

By the time they reached the pinnacle, Adam could barely draw enough breath to fill his lungs. His chest burned and his eyes ached, maybe from the glittering sun on snow. Or perhaps from the spinning in his head. If this was how the horses felt from climbing the mountain, he was grateful he'd not forced his old boy to carry his weight this last hour.

Just ahead, the others had stopped at the edge where the downward slope began. And as Adam stepped up behind them, he knew instantly what had caught their attention.

Vast mountains stretched in every direction as far as he could see. Endless. Huge peaks rose up, then fell away until the next mountain rose again, then the next.

And in the midst of it all, there they stood. The only people who existed anywhere.

The majesty of the scene swelled in his chest, but at the same time, overwhelming loneliness churned in his soul.

How could they ever find a single Blackfoot war party in this territory so immense? They could travel for weeks. Months. Years. And never find another human, much less the kidnappers they sought.

"We have to try." Meksem's voice whispered low, solid as steel. Yet a tinge of fear quivered in her voice. She knew how hopeless their mission seemed.

The desperation she must be feeling wove through his chest, tightening his breathing even more than the climb up the mountain had.

"We're not without hope." Beaver Tail's low murmur sounded so much more certain than Meksem's tone had.

Adam glanced at his friend. The man met his gaze.

"There is a Scripture, 'if God be for us, who can be against us?'" The wisdom glittering in Beaver's dark gaze loosened the strands of fear knotting in Adam's chest. "I know the way to the Blackfoot country. There is one trail that is used most during the cold months." His gaze swung to Meksem. "Your sister is not lost to God. He will show us if we look to Him."

～

*B*eaver Tail's words should have soothed Meksem. He meant them to be reassuring, she had no doubt.

But the fear coursing through her had tightened into bands around her chest at the thought that an all-powerful God had control of the situation. What if she angered Him? What if He didn't like her? Didn't approve of her?

She'd heard of the white man's God. Stories and legends had been told her entire life of how He gave His people great riches. He might love white men and seek to do good things for them, but He knew nothing of her. How could she dare think He might lead her to her sister?

She shook her head. Dwelling on such things would only distract her. The white man's God neither saw nor cared what happened to Telípe.

Meksem straightened and glanced back at Adam and Caleb,

who stood beside their horses. "You ride now?" Surely going downhill wouldn't be too much for their animals.

Adam nodded as he stroked his mount's neck. "He seems to be doing better."

As soon as the two men were mounted, she motioned for Beaver Tail to ride on. The sooner they were underway, the sooner they'd find Telípe. In the meantime, maybe moving would clear her roiling thoughts and ease the fear threatening to strangle her.

This side of the mountain only dipped halfway down before rising again into another peak. The murky light of dusk had begun to settle over them by the time they reached the narrow flat place between the two mountains. Low trees grew in the spot, which would make it a good place to rest.

Should they stop long enough for a short sleep? If they rode on through the night, would Beaver Tail be able to keep them on the right path with only faint moonlight to show the way? She reined her mare beside him.

He threw a look to the low-hanging sky. "We all need to stop and eat. The clouds speak of snow. We don't have time to wait it out, but we can weather the storm better with full bellies and rested horses."

He spoke truth, and her own body strained under exhaustion. She could push herself—she *would* push herself—if she were the only person she had to worry about. But the horses needed rest too.

"I know the trail," Beaver Tail added, "no matter if night or day."

She slid to the ground. "We eat and sleep a little, then ride while still dark." She wouldn't be able to truly rest, for she'd have to make sure they all awakened in the middle of the night to ride again. The way her body felt, if she gave in to her fatigue, she would sleep for days.

Setting up a simple camp didn't take long, but she suspected getting any kind of fire to light would be a challenge. The snow beneath them held a thick crust of ice for them to walk on, but beneath that crust must come up at least to her knees. Digging through the frigid snow would be hard, but, if it could be done, they could use the dry wood they carried with them.

Beaver Tail worked with Susanna on the task. By the time Meksem and the other men had the horses secured and provisions pulled out, they'd built a nice blaze on a raised bed of logs.

Susanna began handing out food, and her husband reached to help with the task. Meksem couldn't keep herself from eyeing him. She'd never seen a brave stoop to woman's work when there was a squaw present to do the task. If anything, he should have looked to Meksem to help Susanna, even though she'd been working alongside the men to care for the animals.

She should assist Susanna anyway, though. "I will help." She reached for the food pack, but the woman waved her away.

"I thought we'd eat what's already cooked." Susanna motioned to the bundles of camas root and roasted meat. "If that's all right, there's nothing more to do." She paused with her brows raised, apparently waiting for Meksem to confirm the plan.

Meksem nodded, but giving her approval seemed strange. Normally she had to fight for a position as equal. Others didn't willingly look to her as a leader.

Susanna's mouth curved into a soft smile. "Sit and rest then."

Meksem took the food the woman offered and pulled a buffalo robe tight around her shoulders. The warm fire soothed her face, bringing her cold-numbed cheeks to life in a painful ache.

Yet it was a good ache. Life slipping back into her frozen limbs.

She let her eyes drift shut, relishing the rich pleasure of warmth. And rest.

Finally.

*E*verything in Adam wanted to pull Meksem close, lay her head on his shoulder, and give her a place to rest.

She sat beside him, her chin dropped to her chest. Sleeping. How could she be getting the deep rest she needed in that uncomfortable position? She pushed herself so hard—too hard. Yet she fought just as fiercely to keep others from taking on some of her burden.

If only he could do something to relieve the weight from her shoulders. But what? He didn't know this country. Beaver Tail was assisting more than anyone. Thankfully, Meksem allowed the brave to lead, trusting in his guidance.

That revealed wisdom on her part. Adam scraped his fingers over his chin, trying to figure something she'd let him do—a way to bear some of her responsibility. Or at least ease her fears.

Almighty God, I know I've not been faithful in prayers or any other acts of devotion, but would You be willing to hear me now?

The prayer slipped through his mind without him planning the words. If the Sovereign God he'd learned about in his youth really was as close as Caleb made Him sound, maybe the Deity would hear him. Would He step in and act?

Adam riffled through the recesses of his memory for some prayer he'd memorized in his school days that might please God. Something that contained the correct words to make the Almighty bend His ear.

I don't know how to ask in the right way, but please aid Meksem. Make this journey easier for her. Show me how to help her.

His gaze shifted to the fire, where the flames had dipped to a small flicker. A glance around the group showed everyone else slept.

Meksem had said she only planned to stay here a few hours. As best he could tell from the scant moonlight, the midnight hour had recently passed. Maybe she wouldn't mind a little while longer before he woke them to start riding again. Surely the sleep would only make them more alert and move faster. He should be dozing too, but in truth, his body seemed to prefer watching her.

As quietly as he could manage, he reached for another log and eased it onto the fire, then added a second. The flame snapped, and Meksem jerked at the sound. Her chin lifted, but her eyes didn't open. Little by little, her head lowered again.

Exhausted.

She worked so hard to be the fierce warrior she thought she had to be, but even this strong woman could only pretend for so long. No one could maintain a façade forever.

He'd learned that lesson the hard way.

~

*A*dam had been right.

Meksem pinched her mouth against the admission. When he woke her just before daylight, she'd been angry with herself for sleeping so long. But he'd said the rest would help them move faster. And he'd spoken true.

She'd never traveled this path Beaver Tail now led them on. Being utterly at his mercy kept her middle in a constant roil, but at least they were covering ground quickly. The horses moved on the ice crust with more energy than they had in days. Perhaps riding through that first night had been the wrong decision. Would they have been better off if she'd allowed them all to sleep?

She would never know for sure.

And besides, a warrior never looked back. Always forward until the journey ended. Then she would speak only the parts of the tale that told of victory. Not all the many, *many* things she wished she'd done differently.

By the time evening fell, her spirit warred within her about whether they should stop for another rest once darkness fell in earnest. The thought of sleeping while Telípe needed her brought a fresh surge of worry—nay, fear—to press hard on her chest. But hadn't she just learned the night before that rest made them travel faster?

Beaver Tail signaled a halt on a section of downhill slope where the ground leveled off a little.

Susanna reached for the tie string on her pack. "Let's eat while the horses rest." Maybe the woman felt the same pinch in her belly that Meksem had for a while now.

Meksem took the baked camas root from Susanna with a nod, and the first bite eased through her, awakening her weary body.

Yet, she didn't miss the way Caleb's face scrunched when he bit into his camas bread. These white men didn't seem to favor the stuff for some reason.

Caleb swallowed his bite quickly. "Any idea if we're catching up to the kidnappers? Or Telípe's husband and his group? What did you say his name was?" He turned the last question to Meksem.

"Heinmot." She glanced in the direction of the setting sun. In truth, she couldn't tell where they were in position to the Salish village Telípe had been taken from.

Farther north, yes. Definitely west. But they'd taken such a roundabout route after the avalanche, she'd lost the landmarks she knew to watch for. "I know not if we're nearing Heinmot's party. He is sick." She shrugged in the sign of one who didn't know the answer. But she didn't let on how the not knowing worried her.

Would Heinmot survive the journey? Did he, even now, lie helpless on a bed of snow on the trail, breathing his last painful breaths? Did he have anyone with him who cared for his well-being?

Telípe would want him to be comfortable if the worst came. The man had been good to her, as far as Meksem knew. Had Telípe been happy in the Salish village?

"Reckon it would be hard to ride through these mountains with all this bone aching snow, and being sick too." Caleb scrunched his nose. "I feel for the man. Is Telípe your only sister?"

Meksem nodded. "One sister, three brothers." She raised three fingers. "They are from my mother's Nimiipuu husband." Why had she said that? She knew better than to give details about her life, especially when they weren't asked for. And it was no business of this man that she'd been born from a different marriage than her younger siblings.

Caleb's brow rose, and she could feel Adam's gaze on her. She didn't glance his way, for he would read more into her words then she wanted him to. He always seemed to see deeper with those orange eyes of his.

"Nimiipuu... That's Nez Perce right? Your pa was from a different tribe?" As deep as Caleb's questions prodded, something in his friendly tone made answering him hard to refuse. In truth, despite his massive frame, Caleb possessed such a genuine kindness, always encouraging and ready to help, she couldn't keep herself from liking him.

So she nodded. "My father was Salish. He died when I was young." Again why did those last words pour from her mouth? More than he'd asked. She sealed her lips shut and raised her gaze to the thick gray sky. "We should ride again. More snow comes." The light dusting that had fallen the night before hadn't been as bad as she'd expected. But the clouds still appeared too heavy.

As Beaver Tail started down the mountain again, she took her place in the rear of the group. This way she could be certain no one straggled behind. Adam rode just in front of her, giving her the perfect view of his spotted gelding, the one who seemed intent on causing trouble.

She couldn't stop the flush of admiration that bloomed in her chest as she watched the animal's sleek muscles dance with each stride. Even its thick winter coat didn't hide the horse's handsome features.

He'd been worth the treasure she traded for him. She swallowed to summon moisture into her dry throat as an image of the tomahawk leapt into her mind.

At least, anyone else would think him equal in value to the heirloom she'd given. With the intricate design carved into its handle, the sparkling green jewels set deep in the rich wood, the chief's eyes had lit when she held it out to him.

Her mind flashed back to the day she'd received the gift. When her father placed the heirloom in her hands, she'd known by the admiration in his eyes the weapon was worth a great deal. He'd never said where the piece came from, only that it was the most special gift he could offer her in his last days.

He'd been wrong though.

The thing she treasured most from her father were the memories she still clutched tight. He'd only been alive through her first five winters, but if she closed her eyes, she could still remember how strong his arms were when they wrapped around her, setting her on his knee at the end of each day. She couldn't remember any of the things he'd told her, but she could still feel the rich vibrato of his voice rumble through her back as she leaned against his chest.

And when he turned her to face him, his eyes had truly seen her. No matter what she tried to hide, he'd seen through her attempts to cover. But even more, he'd seen *why* she hid. No one had ever taken the time to know her like her father had.

Then he'd left. Stolen by a sickness that ravaged their camp.

Leaving her with only the elaborate tomahawk and an empty cavern inside her. Even now, her eyes stung with those memories. This was why she didn't usually let them resurrect.

It seemed trading the tomahawk had stripped her of more than just her father's gift. Now she was losing her inner defenses too.

Her gaze lifted from the spotted horse to the man riding beside him, straight and confident in the saddle. Had gaining his favor been worth the loss of her treasure?

At times like this…she had no idea.

~

"*E*asy, boy. *Tranquilízate, Tesoro.*" Adam stroked the spotted gelding's neck as the animal dozed in the faint light just before dawn. He didn't often speak Spanish anymore, but in this early morning hour, as he breathed the rich scent of horse and wove his fingers through the animal's textured mane, the comfortable words slipped out. "Tesoro."

The gelding lifted his head to look at Adam.

"You like that name?" He rubbed the itchy spot between the animal's eyes. "You are a treasure, no question about it." Maybe this was the name he'd been searching for.

Did Joel ever speak Spanish anymore? He was probably busy

learning the language of his wife to be? Were he and Elan married yet? If her parents accepted him, maybe even today would be their wedding ceremony.

A weight pressed on Adam's chest at the thought of his brother taking such a momentous step without him there to be part of the festivities. But he'd told Joel not to wait on him. He deserved to be happy—to start a new journey with a new partner.

With a final pat on the horse's shoulder, Adam turned away. Better he get moving than dwell on things he had no control over.

As he reached for his saddle, his gaze caught on Caleb's packsaddle. The man had offered its use whenever Adam wanted to try it on the spotted gelding. Today might be a good day to start.

When he approached the horse with the saddle blanket, the gelding flicked an ear toward him to show he was watching but didn't display signs of unease. Not even when Adam stroked the blanket over him, settling the thick cloth in place on his back.

"Well done, Tesoro." He rubbed the horse's neck, then reached for the saddle.

Again, the animal observed with clear interest but didn't seem worried when Adam placed the light saddle frame on his back.

"Good boy." He offered another pat, then loosely cinched the girth in place.

"You will be riding him soon." Meksem's voice slipped over him like a gentle hug as she stepped up beside him.

He couldn't help a glance at her, but then he couldn't make himself turn away. With her strong features and regal bearing, she looked every bit an Indian princess. A princess warrior.

She must have felt his gaze on her, for she turned to him. In the soft light, her dark eyes were hard to read. But he could still see the longing there as she turned away from the horse. And maybe…was that loss? He'd seen that emotion before when she looked at the gelding. What had the animal cost her, and why had she been willing to give up something special for him?

"I love him, Meksem." He put his full heart in his words. "I know you must have traded a great deal for him. I'd like to pay you back." With what, he had no idea. He and Joel hadn't brought anything with them into this wilderness except necessary supplies and horses. But if he could get an idea of what she'd spent, he'd find a way to repay whatever she'd given.

She pulled her gaze from his and stared out into the distance. Beyond the horses, dark fog hid the faraway mountains from view. "I only traded one thing for him. Nothing of value."

But something in her manner appeared forced, as if her words lacked truth. The item must have been of great value. His heart twisted. Why would she do such a thing?

She swung her gaze back to him, her eyes brighter than usual. Maybe a little glassy. "I am glad you like him. When I saw him, I knew he must be yours."

He shifted his attention to the horse and stroked the animal. "His manner reminds me of a stallion we had years ago. Fritz held himself with such an elegant bearing, so much power, and a mind as intelligent as most men's. Everywhere we went, people loved him." He sent her a sideways glance. "He was a good friend."

Her mouth curved in a gentle smile, bringing a softness to her strong features. Stealing his breath. "Like my Apash. We have been together long." She glanced toward her mare, but now Adam couldn't pull his gaze from the woman. Those dark eyes he loved to study, her full lips forming a gentle curve. Her cheeks, her straight nose, her strong jaw—every feature fitting together to form a masterpiece.

Her focus turned back to him, and her brows rose expectantly. Waiting for him to speak?

His mind scrambled for an answer. "Not many people understand how to connect with a horse, and how deep that connection can be. I like that you do." There was so much more he appreciated about her, but even that small comment exposed him.

Her cheeks appled as she dropped her gaze. The look stirred something warm in his belly. He'd never seen her as soft, as innocent, as she seemed now. He wouldn't mind seeing this part of her more often.

As if she read his mind, she raised her chin, squared her shoulders, and then stepped back. "The light comes quickly. We must ride now."

CHAPTER 7

Snow blasted in a fierce gale the entire day, sometimes so thick Meksem could barely see past the horse in front of her. Other times, the flakes tapered enough to make her think they would finally dwindle away.

But then another gust of wind would flare, swirling the snow in a massive wall of white. Even she'd begun shivering by the time true darkness settled over the land that night.

Through the still-falling snow, Beaver Tail's voice called from ahead, signaling a halt. Relief swept through her. Maybe he would insist they stop for the night. Or at least for a few hours to get warm. If he announced that they should rest, she wouldn't have to ask, which would show her weakness against the miserable conditions.

A cliff wall rose up beside them, blocking much of the wind sweeping through the mountains. This might be a good place to rest and start a fire. They'd gathered enough wood the night before and kept it dry in one of the packs, so they should be able to manage a nice warming blaze. Maybe eventually she'd be able to feel her toes again.

She nudged her mare forward to join the group huddled

around Beaver Tail. He looked to her, his dark eyes studying her. "This would be a good place to build a fire and sleep a little?" His tone made the words sound like a question, as though he was seeking her permission.

Before this journey, no brave had ever asked her permission for anything, and it still caught her off guard the way these people looked to her as leader. Part of her wanted to say they should keep riding—the part of her desperate to reach her sister. And maybe the part of her that drove her to be as strong and capable as the other braves.

But he was right. They all desperately needed rest. She nodded her agreement. "We eat. Build fire. Sleep a little."

She dismounted as the others did, but when her feet touched the ground, pain shot through her cold-numbed legs. She gripped her saddle to keep from falling until her limbs gained enough strength to hold her upright.

A grunt from the direction of the others told her at least one of the men suffered the same pain. The thought should make her feel better—she wasn't the only weak one —but she shouldn't be thankful for another's discomfort.

Setting up camp required little effort. No trees provided protection for the animals, so they left the saddles in place, only loosening girths. The blankets and packs would help keep the animals warm.

Once again, Beaver Tail and Susanna built a fire raised on a log bed to keep the layers of snow underneath from snuffing out the flame. After the horses were settled, Meksem gathered with the others around the blaze to eat and soak in the fire's warmth.

They sat closer this night than before, probably because the winds still snaked icy fingers around them. The rock wall assisted on one side, but not having trees as a buffer allowed the breeze too much freedom.

On one side of Meksem, Susanna tucked close to her

husband, sharing a buffalo robe wrapped around both their shoulders. The hide's thick hair brushed against Meksem's own buffalo covering as she tucked her fur close around her shoulders and over her head.

On her other side, Adam sat wrapped in an elk fur. The hide must have been from a female, for it was only large enough to wrap his upper body. He'd laid a wolf skin across his lap, but the combination must not be sufficient, for his hands trembled like leaves quivering in the wind.

Before she could let herself think too much about what she was doing, she opened one side of her buffalo robe and held it out to him. "Wrap this around your shoulders. Warmer with two."

Surprise slipped across his face for only an instant before he took the edge she offered and pulled the fur around him. He scooted close enough for their arms and legs to touch, and she had to force herself not to jolt at the contact.

She might have questioned his eagerness to join with her, except that the quivering in his body set her own limbs trembling. The man was half frozen.

"Here, spread this across your lap too." He lifted one side of his wolf fur.

She shook her head to refuse. He needed the warmth much more than she did, and she wasn't sure her awakening nerves could handle being any closer to this man. Her body hummed with awareness of him.

But before she could resist, he spread the soft hide over her legs and pulled the buffalo robe close around them again.

As silence settled over the group, she focused on slow, even breaths while she stared into the fire. Every part of her had sprung to life with this man so near, much like that day of the avalanche when he rode behind her on her horse.

She'd never allowed herself to get too close to the other braves she traveled with on hunting parties, but if she'd held to that notion now, there could have been dire consequences. He could have frozen as the night grew colder.

She couldn't let him suffer, even if helping him required getting too close. This man affected her more than any brave ever had. Made her feel so alive at times her blood raced through her neck.

Yet his nearness made her want more. When he looked at her, he seemed to see her. He even seemed to accept the parts of her she hated. That feeling of being known had scared her at first, but the more time she spent around him, the more of him she craved. At first, her longings had been only for his attention, but now, with his leg pressed against hers, she realized his touch could easily become intoxicating.

The others spoke a little as they finished eating, and Caleb added more wood to the fire before they all settled into sleeping positions.

Adam had finally stopped shivering beside her, but she didn't dare take the buffalo robe away from him.

He glanced sideways at her. "You can lay your head on my shoulder to sleep if you want." Under the fur, he moved his hand to tap his shoulder, and in the process his fingers brushed her arm.

Again, she had to force herself not to jump at the contact. She shook her head. "I can sleep sitting up."

His lips tipped in what might have been a smile, but, with the firelight reflecting in his eyes, she couldn't tell for sure. "I know you can, but it might be more comfortable to lean against something."

She could only imagine how pleasing resting against Adam would feel, but there was no way she would allow herself the luxury. Perhaps she should offer him the same, yet she couldn't bring herself to suggest he draw closer. He might actually take her up on the idea.

She let her head drop forward as she usually did when

preparing to sleep upright, but she wouldn't be able to doze off with him so near. At least she could rest. Renew her strength for the next long ride.

~

*M*eksem awoke finally warm.

She'd been cold for so many days, this pocket of heat felt like she'd finally reached the afterlife, a place filled with the glorious warmth of the great sun. Something pressed on top of her head, but not so heavy as to be painful.

She opened her eyes, fighting against the hold of exhaustion. Darkness wrapped around her.

Not the sunny afterlife.

Her fingers brushed against fur. Realization swept through her, replacing some of her pleasure. She must be tucked inside the cocoon of her fur blanket. They'd been on the trail of the war party that kidnapped Telípe.

The fur over her head shifted, and she stiffened. Had she fallen asleep atop her horse? Then, the pressure on her head lifted.

In that instant, the true situation rushed in. The last thing she could remember was sitting beside Adam, wrapped with him in the buffalo robe.

She straightened, pushing herself upright, fumbling with the furs to find their opening. Warm breath brushed against her cheek, and panic sluiced through her. She pushed away from the body that must be Adam. Had she slept cradled in his arms?

"It's all right, Meksem. Only me." Adam's rumble did nothing to calm her.

At last, she found the opening in the fur and threw her side away. Cold slapped her face, knocking some sense back into her. She sat upright, breaths coming through jagged inhales.

A warrior didn't panic, even when she found herself

wrapped in the arms of an attractive fellow traveler. Sleeping on that man's chest. The heat flooding her face did an excellent job of warding off the icy wind.

"Here. Take the buffalo fur back." Adam pulled the thick hide away from him and tried to wrap it around her shoulders.

She shook her head. "We need to ride." A glance at the sky revealed the darkness turning to light. She sprang to her feet. "Wake the others and pack camp. I'll ready the horses." She had to get away from this man's befuddling presence. A warrior needed all of her senses to stay strong.

Especially on a mission like this one.

~

Adam leaned forward in his saddle as his gelding crested a low hill, Tesoro stepping nimbly at his side. This was the gelding's second day carrying the packsaddle, and Adam had gradually tightened the girth to full tension. The animal had settled in well, not causing a bit of trouble. A nice change from those earlier episodes.

Hard riding each day had strengthened Tesoro's lean muscle, and the animal's winter coat shone in the sunlight.

If only they could all thrive as well as the spotted gelding was.

His gaze wandered up the line of riders in front of him. Meksem had announced that Adam should take the rear guard today, then stationed herself near the front. She still let Beaver Tail lead, and Susanna rode just behind him in the wife's place, but Meksem took up the spot behind her. That left Caleb and French as a buffer between Adam and the woman who seemed determined to keep her distance after that morning's debacle.

Watching her fall asleep last night had formed a knot in his chest, especially when she wouldn't even trust him enough to use his shoulder for a pillow.

But sometime after he finally dozed off, his body had jerked to life as she leaned sideways to rest her arm against his. He'd barely breathed when her head lowered to lay on his shoulder.

She must not have realized what she'd done.

He hadn't planned to touch her, at least not with his hands, but when her head dropped forward and she started to fall over, he wrapped his arm around her shoulders and pulled her close. He'd slept like a hibernating bear from that point on, with her snuggled in his arms.

Until she woke up.

At first he'd thought she would ease away to protect her dignity. But there had been no question which moment she realized she lay in his arms. He'd been lucky she hadn't slapped him before she scrambled away.

As the day progressed, he'd spent far too many hours reliving all those memories—the ones filled with pure pleasure, and those where she'd stabbed the knife in his chest and twisted.

Her rejection didn't bother him as much as the way she fought so hard against letting everyone in. Or maybe she was simply disgusted by him. Maybe the connection he felt all those times had been on his part only. Maybe her incredible thoughtfulness in giving him the spotted gelding had simply been a sign of her generosity.

Maybe he should stop reading so much into her actions.

But that wouldn't stop every part of him from longing to know her better. To be the one she allowed past her defenses.

Beaver Tail's voice drifted from in front of them, and his hand rose to call a halt.

Adam nudged his horses closer to hear what the man had to say. They'd only been riding an hour since they stopped for lunch, so surely this wasn't another rest.

Beaver sent a look at the three mountains in front of them. "I need to scout ahead. I remember one of the passes was too hard to travel, so we came back through the other one. I don't remember which is the better." He looked to Meksem. "Follow until you reach the two rocks stacked on top of each other. Wait for me there."

When she nodded, Beaver Tail turned his attention to his wife. As he rode his horse alongside hers, Adam looked away. It must be hard to be a newly married couple on the trail with a group like theirs. No privacy for...the things married people did. As uncomfortable as their long looks and occasional kisses made the rest of the party, he didn't begrudge the pair.

He just didn't want to watch them.

After a long moment, Beaver Tail turned his horse and rode away at a lope. Adam finally returned his gaze to their group.

Susanna stared after her husband with a lovesick look, the corners of her mouth tipping into a smile. Any man would be lucky to have a woman stare after him that way.

As much as Adam tried to fight it, he couldn't stop his gaze from drifting to Meksem. She certainly wasn't the type of woman to watch her man ride away with that smitten expression on her face.

The time had passed for him to face the truth.

Pining after her would only lead to disappointment. He needed to put distance between them, as she'd done today. Even more than she'd done.

But when her eyes lifted to meet his look, a flash of vulnerability there reached into his chest and gripped him. Getting over this woman would be no easy thing. Especially when every part of him wanted to take on the challenge she offered.

She would be worth the effort to win her heart, he had no doubt.

CHAPTER 8

They needed to move on. Waiting for Beaver Tail's return beside the two boulders had bound Meksem's restless muscles in knots.

Meksem could only keep herself from pacing when she sat, so she forced herself to stay propped against the lower rock. They'd all dismounted to let the horses rest, and after Beaver Tail didn't return right away, they loosened the animals' girths and gave them fodder to munch on. At least the horses would benefit from the delay.

She sent another glance up the mountainside, first to the pass between the right mountain and the middle, then to the gap between the middle peak and the crest on the left.

Enough snow-covered rocks and scraggly trees littered the mountainside to hide Beaver Tail from view soon after he'd started toward the pass on the right.

Had he only explored one side so far? Surely he would know from investigating that pass whether that was the course they should travel or if the other route would be better.

A nicker jerked her gaze to a snow-covered rock just in front of them. Beaver Tail and his horse appeared from behind the stone, the man leaning forward in the saddle to give the gelding freedom to climb the icy incline.

The expression on his face gave away none of his findings. But when he reached them, he nodded. "That is the best way."

Expelling a relieved breath, Meksem stepped to her horse's side, tightened the cinch, and swung her leg over the saddle. At last, they could return to their search. The others followed her example, and in the space of a few breaths they'd gone from impatiently waiting to moving again. Finally.

They covered the next section of trail faster than any they'd traveled that morning, following the prints Beaver Tail's horse had just made. First down a short stretch, then climbing steeply to the place the two mountains met. The pass between them stood narrow and thick with snow, but the crust of ice atop the layers looked thick enough to keep the horses from breaking through.

"The other pass does not have level ground to ride on." Beaver Tail's voice drifted from ahead. "The mountains meet in sharp points. Too steep for horses." He held his hands in a V to show the slope.

How would they ever have managed this journey without Beaver Tail? She was more than grateful she hadn't insisted he stay behind.

French's packhorse stumbled as they maneuvered through the pass. But the animal stayed upright, and they descended the slope down the other side without event.

At the bottom of the mountain, a level section stretched out before them, wider than anything they'd seen since entering the mountain country days before.

"Lookee there." Caleb's tone rose with enthusiasm. "I spy a good stretch to run." He sent a grin back at Adam. "Too bad that colt's not riding yet. Want to try him out here?"

The thought turned Meksem's belly. An unwanted image emerged of the horse tearing across the flat land, bucking like a savage beast. Adam's body flying through the air, smacking the hard ground. Lying lifeless in the snow.

A horrible thought, yet, even so, something more disturbed her spirit. Something about the valley ahead didn't feel right.

She scanned the flat stretch nestled with mountains rising up on all sides. Just like…

"Wait." She jerked her mare to a stop.

Adam seemed the only one to hear her. When he glanced back and saw her paused, his voice boomed loudly. "Halt!"

That brought the group to a quick standstill, and she turned her gaze to the level ground ahead to confirm that her suspicions were right. They had to be. "That's a lake, frozen over. The ice might not yet be strong."

The others followed her focus, and, a heartbeat later, Adam's voice sounded again. "She's right. I don't know why I didn't see it earlier."

"You'd think after falling through ice once, you'd grow a sixth sense about that stuff." Caleb's words were light, but his tone murmured low enough to make it clear he knew the gravity of the situation they'd almost ridden into.

Beaver Tail motioned to their left. "The animals have made a path around this edge." He turned to Meksem with raised brows.

She studied the trail, then nodded. "The animals know best." She still felt like she was dreaming every time one of these people looked to her for guidance. Especially the Blackfoot warrior in the lead.

They'd only gone a few steps when Beaver Tail reined his horse off the trail and halted. His eyes fixed on the ground, and he nudged his gelding forward a few slow steps.

Tracks formed a line across the snow, and she guided her mare around Susanna's to better see them. Mountain goats had come through here recently, maybe earlier that day.

Then her gaze caught what Beaver Tail must see also.

Horse prints. A great many of them.

The tracks crossed the path, coming from the direction of the left pass—the one they hadn't taken—and crossed the game trail, moving out onto the frozen lake. There were at least—she guided her mare the direction the prints came from—at least four horses. No, five.

Was this Heinmot's group?

"Think this is your sister's husband?" Adam must have listened to her thoughts.

She scanned the tracks as far as she could see them across the lake. "I don't—"

A dark spot in the snow gripped her chest, stealing her breath. She pointed, her mind whirling too much to find the white man's word to say *look!*

The ice... Was it broken? Had one of the horses fallen through?

"Dear, Lord, no. Please don't let it be." Susanna rode up beside Meksem, shielding her eyes from the sun as she studied the distant spot.

"I can't see for certain from here. Let's ride around and get a better look." Beaver Tail nudged his horse forward along the game trail.

The others fell in behind him, and the path was wide enough for two or three to ride abreast. Meksem found herself beside Susanna. Thankfully, the woman didn't speak. Meksem's mind roiled so much, words would have only muddied her thoughts.

As they made their way around the snow-covered lake, what must have happened soon became clear. The dark spot in the snow looked to be near the center, and, though she couldn't tell whether the ice was broken in that area, so much snow was disturbed, something had definitely happened there. The hoof prints leading away took a slightly different angle. As though the riders were simply trying to reach the nearest shore, not worrying about a straight line.

When they met the tracks on the far side of the lake, the prints faded into an area of churned snow. Two places had pressed down, as though people had sat, maybe to warm themselves after falling through the ice?

No matter what had occurred, the riders had eventually traveled onward.

"Those prints look fresh. How long ago do you think they came through here?" French peered at the tracks leading toward the mountains ahead of them.

The solid edges of ice around each hoof hadn't melted or filled with new snow. No animals had trod over them either.

"I'd say sometime today. Maybe this morning early." Beaver Tail stared toward the mountain in front of them. "They're going the same direction we're headed."

"Seems there's a chance it could be your sister's husband, right?" French looked to her, brows raised.

Meksem gave a slow nod. "A chance." This wasn't the path she knew from Heinmot's village to the Blackfoot country, but maybe they'd been blown off course too. Perhaps one of them knew the same route Beaver Tail was leading them on.

Beaver straightened in his saddle. "Let's get moving then. Maybe we can catch them by dark."

Susanna motioned for Meksem to ride behind Beaver Tail. "You'll probably want to see the tracks too."

Meksem sent her a thankful nod. Not many people focused on others' needs as much as this woman. As unlikely a pair as she and Beaver Tail had seemed at first, they fit well together, each bringing unique strengths and talents. And the love between them was evident in every look and touch, even in the air around them.

The group pushed hard until dark but didn't catch up with the riders they were tracking. From the horse droppings along the way, the other group looked to be at least half a day ahead.

Maybe they could close the distance through the night.

As they followed a somewhat level goat trail around the mountain, Beaver Tail glanced back at her. "I don't remember how far to the next valley. Should we keep riding or stop to sleep a few hours?"

Weariness tugged on her body, but they still had so much ground to cover. The only way they would catch up to the group ahead of them would be to keep going. And they still didn't know how far ahead the Blackfoot war party was. The horses seemed able to keep moving, especially since most of them had rested while they waited for Beaver Tail earlier.

She set her jaw. "Keep riding."

Was she making the right decision? The balance between pushing too hard and not hard enough felt like teetering on the sharp edge of a mountain peak. With all these lives in her care—including her sister and the other captives—she couldn't make a mistake.

~

"Hello, Tesoro." Adam let the spotted gelding sniff his hand the next morning in the predawn darkness.

The horse snuffled a greeting, then raised his muzzle for Adam to blow into each nostril in the usual way horses greeted each other. After a friendly snort, the horse dropped his head and smacked his lips in a contented gesture.

"Good, boy." Adam stroked the gelding's neck. "Think you're ready this morning?"

The horse had been doing so well with the packsaddle and the weight Adam added little by little. Tesoro gave easily to pressure on his halter, and more importantly, he was developing the trust so important between the two of them. He hadn't spooked at all yesterday, and the two times he'd been nervous, he'd leaned his head against Adam's leg in the stirrup and seemed to take comfort in the steady pressure. Exactly what they'd been working toward.

"Let's try it then." Adam eased his riding saddle onto the gelding's back, then tightened the cinch a little at a time, like he did with the packsaddle. He didn't worry about the bridle, just tied the rope on either side of the halter. First, the horse could get accustomed to a rider, then later Adam would introduce the bit.

As he led the gelding away from the tie line to an open place where they could work, he sent a glance toward the campfire where the others still slept. He'd added more wood to build up the blaze, and these few minutes before dawn would be just enough time for him to work with the gelding.

When he reached the open spot, he took a few minutes to stroke the gelding. "All right, boy. We'll start with a little weight. You'll see this is nothing to worry over." He kept up a steady murmur as he leaned his arms across the saddle, putting as much weight in the center as he could with his feet still on the ground. Then he placed his left foot in the stirrup and pushed down, a little at a time. The horse shuffled its feet for better balance but didn't show signs of nervousness.

"Well done. Now a little more." Adam used the stirrup to push himself up so his belly rested on the saddle. Again Tesoro shifted his hooves for better balance. He raised his nose a little, ears directed toward Adam as if trying to determine what he was doing.

"You're fine. Doing better than Fritz did, that's for certain." He kept up his crooning as he wiggled in the saddle, letting the horse feel his shifting.

A rush of nerves tightened his muscles as he prepared to ease himself up into a sitting position. So far, the horse hadn't even tried to step forward. Adam had prepared for so much worse than this, but Tesoro was proving all of Adam's work so far had been worth the time and effort.

Without daring a breath, Adam lifted himself into the saddle and lowered his right leg on the horse's other side. No quick movements, just steady shifting.

Underneath him, Tesoro tensed, his muscles coiling. His ears twitched in quick flicks.

Adam started up his crooning again. "Easy boy. Settle down now." He forced himself to breathe out, then in again in a steady rhythm. If he let his body tighten, the horse would feel his nerves and feed off them.

A sharp snap sounded in the trees near their camp, and the gelding jerked.

Adam tensed, securing his legs around the horse, balancing himself deep in the saddle in case the animal darted forward.

For a moment, the horse froze. Then he sprung sideways.

Not the direction Adam had prepared for.

He gripped the saddle with one hand and the rope with the other, pulling hard on the halter. "Whoa!"

Tesoro knew the verbal command, but in his panic, he didn't seem to be listening. As he shot toward a cluster of trees, Adam gave another hard yank on the rope. "Ho."

The horse charged through the pressure, and Adam changed to a sideways pull, working to turn the animal's nose. If his head turned, the rest of his body would follow, slowing his forward movement and giving Adam a way to get his attention. To still the panic.

He pulled with all his might toward the left, and the animal finally started to give.

Then another horse raised a shrill whinny.

The cry sent Tesoro into a new frenzy. He lunged forward, jerking the rope out of Adam's hand. His back hooves slipped in the snow, and, for an awful second, the horse's feet flailed like he was going down. A frantic fall like this could easily break the animal's leg.

But Tesoro righted himself, scrambling to gain traction in the icy snow. With a half buck, he catapulted forward.

Maybe it was the horse's sudden movement, or maybe Adam's limbs were too numb to keep a tight grip. His fingers slid on the leather, slipping away as the saddle pulled out from under him.

In the next moment, he was airborne.

*A*dam's back landed hard on the horse's rump, and the animal's forward movement flipped him in a backwards somersault. His face hit the ground half a heartbeat before his belly and feet struck the thick ice crust over the snow.

His lungs squeezed, refusing to let in air as terror welled in his throat. *Calm down.* He'd had the air knocked out of him many times, enough to know he'd be able to breathe faster if he didn't panic.

But his body screamed for air. He struggled for even a little breath.

Voices clamored in the distance. The high neigh of a frightened horse.

The world around him dimmed to a thin circle of light. At last, a tiny stream of air filtered down his throat. He struggled for another. Breath after breath, his head finally cleared.

Tesoro.

He pushed himself up to his knees and blinked in the dim morning light as he struggled to bring the world into focus.

Across the distance, Meksem was easing toward Tesoro, who stood huddled beside a cliff wall.

Beaver Tail and French approached the horse on either side of her, spread apart to cut off the animal's retreat if he tried to run.

"Are you hurt?" Susanna crouched beside him and laid a tentative hand on his shoulder. "Can you sit and catch your breath?"

He was still on his hands and knees, drawing in thick gulps of air, and his chest and throat burned from the icy breaths. His limbs threatened to give way underneath him, so he obeyed her request. He could sit to recover while Meksem brought the gelding back.

But when he twisted and sank onto the ground, a shot of fire ran from his hip up his lower back. A groan slipped out before he could stop it.

Not again. How had he let this happen? Just when his hind parts had finally stopped aching.

And this pain was so much worse than before.

"What's wrong, Adam? Where do you hurt? Is it your back?"

He bit down on another groan. "Not hurt." He moved his hand to his hip, holding pressure there to ease the throbbing.

"He finally got you, huh?" Caleb appeared behind Susanna, his massive frame towering over them both. "What happened?"

"Thought I'd ride him a few minutes before we break camp for the day. Something spooked him. A tree branch, I think." Or maybe a log snapping in the fire, he'd never know for sure.

And the cause didn't matter. What mattered was that the horse hadn't trusted him. This kind of fall happened when he rushed things.

Across the way, Meksem had caught the gelding and was leading him back. Now that the horse was safe, everything in Adam wanted to lie back in the snow and let the ice numb the fire inside him.

But if he did that, the others would realize how much pain he was in. The men would joke and the women would hover.

Well, maybe not Meksem. She didn't seem like the hovering sort. She seemed more like the sort to be cross over him causing a delay.

Locking his jaw against the pain, he pushed himself to his knees again, then worked himself up to standing. He didn't draw breath until he'd fully straightened.

As Meksem strode near with the horse, she studied him with a gaze that seemed to see all the stiffness he was trying to hide. He reached for the reins, doing his best not to let the heat crawling up his neck show on his face. Falling off a horse always bruised a man's pride, and much more in front of a woman.

Especially *this* woman, who rode as if she'd been born on horseback. At least she didn't ask him why he'd been riding the young gelding alone in the dark. Her gaze softened as she handed him the rope.

"Thanks for catching him." His throat went dry just thinking about the possibility of losing this special horse in the mountain wilderness. He swallowed to summon moisture so he could speak again. "We're ready to break camp?" By this time the last few mornings, they'd been in the saddle already.

"Come eat first." She spoke as if impatience didn't claw in her chest.

In fact, the gentleness in her gaze soothed away a little of his pain. At least, the pain in his spirit, if not that in his body.

He turned his focus to Tesoro, who now stood beside him with his head lowered in a drowsy pose. He stroked the horse's neck. "Sorry, old boy. Guess I rushed things."

The horse leaned into his touch. One would never know he'd exploded only moments before like a mountain lion was attacking.

Adam eased out a breath, letting the last half hour slip out of him with the spent air. They had to cover a lot of ground today, and he couldn't slow them down with his impulsive desires and adventures. Meksem was counting on him. He couldn't fail in his responsibilities…not this time.

~

Meksem knew better than anyone how quickly life could be snuffed out.

She inhaled a slow, deep breath, then exhaled. Yet the intentional breathing didn't loosen the knots coiling tightly in her shoulders as she rode.

From the moment she'd heard Adam's hard grunt that morning, the thud of his body slamming on the icy ground, her insides had been balled tight.

What if he'd been truly hurt when the horse spooked? What if he'd been killed, his neck snapped as he tumbled backward off the animal? Those rear hooves could've slammed into him, destroying his body and cutting off the life of a man she'd let herself become far too attached to.

The last time she'd loved a man so freely, he'd died, taken by the sicknesses that swept their camp. The pain had overwhelmed her when her father breathed his last, even though she'd only been five winters old. She'd promised she would never let herself feel that awful again.

But the terror slicing through her this morning when she saw Adam lying face down on the ground had felt too much like those dark days so many years ago.

She tried another deep breath, forcing the tension from her chest as she blew out a cloud of white.

Adam still lived. Hopefully, the pain from his fall would subside.

This time, he'd been spared. Maybe his God had allowed the fall as a warning to her. A reminder not to let herself get too close.

She straightened in the saddle, forcing her shoulders to relax. A warning she would take to heart.

"Tracks again." From the front of the group, Beaver Tail motioned to the snow beside him.

Her heart leapt. The wind through the night had blown snow over the prints from the group they were following. Finding fresh markings would be helpful.

"These are from today." She scanned the sharp lines of the hoof prints. "Must have camped near here."

"Let's move faster. Maybe we can catch them." Adam spoke aloud the nudging in her chest.

Beaver Tail nodded. "We can trot once we pass that rock."

Soon, they pushed the horses into a steady jog. On some animals, the gait jolted enough to loosen a person's teeth, but Apash possessed smooth rhythm Meksem could ride for hours.

A glance back at Adam sent a spear of worry through her. His face had twisted into a miserable grimace, and he clutched his saddle as though trying to keep his back from shaking with the bumping of his horse.

Was he injured worse from his fall then she'd thought?

"Whoa." She raised her voice loud enough for Beaver Tail to hear.

He glanced back as he slowed his horse, his brows raised in question.

She lifted her chin. "Better to walk. Ground too rough." Adam wouldn't appreciate his pain being called out.

Beaver Tail nodded, but a line still formed in his brow. When he turned forward again, she slid a glance back to check on Adam. He slumped in the saddle, still gripping the leather. His mask of agony had slipped to pain-lined exhaustion.

Had he broken a bone? What could she do if he had? Whatever he suffered from, the injury wasn't obvious, not like blood gushing from a wound or a broken arm. She needed to question him. If he pushed too hard with something very wrong inside him, he could suffer a fate so much worse than pain in the saddle.

As they wound over thick, rocky hills, skirting the base of first one mountain then the next, her mind churned. What was Telípe doing right now? Did her belly gnaw with hunger? Did she limp with bruises from the abuse of her captors? Did the baby still grow within her?

Longing ached in Meksem's chest. If only there truly was a God able to see and protect Telípe until Meksem could get there. If only the white man's God were real and cared about the Nimíipuu and Salish people too.

Meksem felt so weak, no matter how strong and capable she tried to be. No matter how hard she worked, she might not reach Telípe in time. In truth, she may not find her at all. If only Telípe had an all-powerful God she could turn to.

At last, they reached an ice-covered stream in a narrow valley.

"Let's stop and eat while the horses drink and rest." Beaver Tail reined in his gelding and swung down to the ground.

While the rest of them loosened cinches and settled the horses, Susanna—the keeper of the food pack—pulled out camas bread and began handing the food out.

Adam led his geldings to the water with a slow stiffness, almost hobbling. The sight pressed a pain in Meksem's chest as she followed with her mare. At the water's edge, Apash dipped her nose into the creek and gulped eagerly, and Meksem couldn't stop her gaze from shifting to Adam beside her. "You are hurting." She spoke the words softly enough the others wouldn't hear.

"Just stiff." He might have meant his tone to be casual, but the words held a forced edge. As though even speaking took painful effort.

How could she find out the truth of his condition? Maybe if

she pushed hard enough that he realized she wouldn't relent. "Are bones broken?"

He shifted his weight, and a flash of pain crossed his face with the movement. "Just bruises, I think."

"I do not have the bark of willow to stop the pain. Maybe Susanna does."

He shook his head. "I won't slow us down. Don't worry about me."

The words reached into her chest and twisted. How could she not worry about him? Concern for this man had taken root inside her, no matter how she tried to stop it.

A sluice of anger washed through her. She hated not having power over her emotions, and this man seemed to draw her out against her will.

"Whether I worry about you or not, I would not have you hurting. This journey is important, but I will not risk your life." She forced herself to breathe with slow, steady inhales.

His eyes widened, and she replayed her words in mind. Had she given away her yearnings? No. At least, not unless he read more into her statements than she'd meant to say. Or maybe he thought her so focused on rescuing Telípe, she cared nothing for the lives of the people in her care.

A new pain pressed her chest. Did they think her so selfish? So driven? Even Adam? She worked so hard to be as tough as the other warriors, but did that mean she had to be cruel also? Couldn't there be a balance?

"Meksem." Adam spoke her name in a gentle voice that drew her from the painful churning of her thoughts.

When she met his gaze, his eyes had softened, seeing deep inside her in that special way only he could do. A stinging crept into her own eyes, a sensation she hadn't felt in so long. Hadn't *allowed* herself to feel. This man flayed her, making her lose the control she fought so hard for.

And the worst part about it...a little bit of her wanted to open herself to him. To let him take some of her burden.

Could she? Would lowering her defenses be so wrong? She pressed her lips together to keep from saying something she would regret. But then her mouth trembled.

"Meksem." Again Adam used that soft tone, but this time his voice gave her courage.

She summoned her inner strength as she met his gaze. "It matters to me if you're hurt, Adam. If there's something I can do for you—to help you—please tell me." This time she spoke the words without anger.

His gaze held hers gently, like a caress. "Thank you. I'm sore, but I can keep riding." Then the corners of his eyes crinkled in the makings of a smile. "As long as we don't trot again. I wasn't sure I could stand that a minute longer."

The humor in his words slipped the weight of worry off her chest, leaving her light enough that she almost laughed. The smile tugging felt so foreign, but good. "No more trotting."

*A*pash's ears pricked, alerting Meksem to danger ahead. She scanned the wooded landscape before her, searching for some clue of what spooked the horse. Beaver Tail's shoulders tensed at the same time, and he jerked his mount to a halt as he raised a silent hand for the others to do the same.

A faint orange glow seeped around the edge of the mountainside about twenty strides ahead, and the scent of wood fire drifted on the air. Meksem's pulse thrummed in her veins. They'd caught up to the riders they'd been following. A group of five, according to their tracks. Hopefully, Heinmot would be among them.

Meksem slid off Apash and crept forward. She should be the one to approach them. If these were Salish, they were her people. She would be the one to speak their language. Beaver Tail would only draw their arrows.

Motioning with her head to signal her intentions, she handed her reins to Susanna and eased forward on silent feet. When she reached the boulder blocking her view of their camp, she paused and pressed her back against the rock, then leaned to peek around. The crackle of the fire sounded from around the stone.

The party must have tucked their camp in the crook of the boulder, away from the wind. Not a wise move if they were worried about others sneaking up on them, but they must have thought no one would dare venture into these mountains in the peak of winter.

A voice murmured, and she could just make out the rhythm of the Salish tongue, but not any specific words.

This had to be Heinmot and his group. She eased forward enough to see them, keeping herself hidden as much as possible.

Four men sat around a small campfire. As she scanned for the fifth, she squinted at a pile of furs that appeared to be stacked bedding. Black hair crowned the end, and a man's eyes peeked just below the locks.

Heinmot? Whether this was her sister's husband or not, the man lay huddled under the pelts, curled in a tight ball.

The others were eating, mostly staring into the fire. One of them looked barely older than a boy, two others possessed the white hair of the aged, and she could only see the back of the fourth man. His profile looked more like that of a young warrior. Maybe Heinmot's younger brother?

She'd never met him, but Telípe had spoken of the man. The younger brother was closer to Telípe's age, and Meksem had the feeling her sister would have preferred marriage to him.

But Heinmot had been the one to ask, and he'd paid the price her father requested in trade. The few times she'd seen her sister after the marriage, Telípe had spoken kindly of her husband. Hopefully, he'd been good to her.

Meksem's belly knotted as her gaze slipped back to the man lying down. That had to be Heinmot. So sick, how could he save her sister from the fierce Blackfoot warriors?

Renewed purpose surged through her veins.

She made the call of a sparrow, an animal they would know

didn't live in these mountains, especially at night. She had no desire to be shot when she stepped into their firelight.

The men spun in her direction, and she stepped away from the rock, revealing herself. She made the sign for peace as she approached near enough to speak in a normal tone.

The man lying on the ground lowered his fur enough so she could see his face. Despite the hollow cheeks and skin hanging in thick wreaths around his jowls, she would know her sister's husband anywhere. Shadows hid his eyes, so she couldn't tell if he recognized her or not.

"I am Meksem, the sister of Telípe." She spoke in her strong warrior voice.

The younger brave, the one who'd been sitting with his back to her before, glanced at Heinmot, then addressed her. "You ride alone?" His eyes seemed almost mocking, as though she must be half-witted to traipse these treacherous mountains on her own.

"I ride with others." She motioned in the direction where the rest of her group waited. "We seek the Blackfoot dogs who took my sister."

Heinmot lowered his fur covering more and looked as if he wished he could sit up. How could he even ride a horse in this weakened state?

"Come and sit." His voice graveled, thick with sludge.

She hadn't planned to stop for a half-night's rest yet, but she had to see the truth of Heinmot's condition. Maybe she and the others could rest here a while, then ride through the final part of the dark hours. "I will bring those who travel with me."

"Bring them." The young brave rose to his feet and took up a position where he would better see anyone coming.

As she turned back the way she'd come, she didn't miss the man's hand moving to rest on the handle of his tomahawk.

Adam met her as soon as she rounded the boulder. "Is it Telípe's husband?"

She nodded as the others crowded near. "We are to sit at

their fire and talk. Heinmot looks very weak. I will try to send him home while we go on." The idea hadn't even settled in her thoughts before it slipped from her mouth, but the notion felt right.

He would see they were capable of winning Telípe and the other captives back. Meksem had as much desire to see her sister home safe as Heinmot did.

Adam touched her arm, a reassuring weight. "I'm sure he'll see what's best."

She took her horse's reins from Susanna and led their group around the giant rock to enter the firelight. The Salish group watched in silence as her party filed into view. One of the older men pointed into the darkness past the firelight. "Nazog will help you see to your horses."

A boy stepped in the direction the man pointed, and Meksem turned to her group to translate the Salish words into the white tongue.

Adam stepped beside her. "Let me take your horse." He kept his voice low, for her ears alone.

She met his gaze. "We can take our night's rest around their fire, but we must ride again long before daylight."

His eyes said he understood well, even before he nodded. "I agree."

When she placed her reins in his hand, even the brush of her glove against his sent warmth up her arm. She had to force her mind to focus as she turned back to Heinmot and the three men standing around him.

The younger brave spoke first. "I am Alahmoot, the brother of Heinmot. This is Ukugnut, whose daughter was taken. And Yaka, who comes to win back his wife and boy child."

Upon hearing the names, she peered closer at the first man Alahmoot pointed to. Ukugnut meant *bald* in the Salish tongue, and when he shifted, the firelight glimmered off bare skin atop his head. He must have been renamed later in life, as was often done.

Poor fellow. The People often had ten or more names throughout their lives, reflecting some great event or character trait, but surely Ukugnut hadn't chosen this particular title.

The other man Alahmoot had motioned toward—Yaka, if she'd heard correctly—looked to be the oldest in the group. Yet apparently his wife was young enough to have a small son. Not surprising, as many Salish men took much younger wives, but seeing him made her thankful once again her own mother and stepfather hadn't forced her to marry against her will.

She certainly didn't desire the life of a squaw.

She'd rather lead a hunting party any day than cook for an old man she barely knew. And she had no wish to warm his bed. She pushed the thoughts away before heat climbed up her neck and stole her control.

"Sit." Heinmot's voice dragged with weariness.

The two elders obeyed, and Meksem took up a place across from them. Alahmoot stayed where he stood, and she couldn't blame him. She would have been leery to sit with so many strangers around, especially those tending the horses in the darkness where he couldn't see them.

She would introduce her group when they returned from tending the horses, but for now, she focused on Heinmot and watched his reaction as she spoke her next words. "I have been told my sister carries your child."

Worry tightened the sagging skin around his mouth. "That is true. If they both still live."

That same worry swirled in Meksem's belly. "I will not rest until I see my sister safe again." She leveled a piercing look on the man. "You have my word. But I need to move fast. Those with me have pledged to help."

Alahmoot stiffened. "Is that not a Blackfoot you ride with? I see their markings on his horse, and he has the look of those savages."

Meksem worked hard to school her features as she nodded. "He is Blackfoot, but he will fight against those who steal our women. He will do all in his power to help. I trust him."

As she spoke the assurance, the truth of her statements settled in her chest with certainty. She did trust the man. He'd proven himself over and over. In truth, she trusted him more than the brave who faced her, eyeing her with disdain.

"What would a woman know of a man such as him?" The censure in eyes shouldn't surprise her.

She'd seen the same look from so many braves through the years. In time, she would prove herself to this man as she'd done with the others. The first step would be in not allowing herself to react to his demeaning words.

She turned to Heinmot. "We will rest a little this night, then ride on while still dark. You do not look well. Let me pursue those who took my sister. Go to your village and recover. I will bring her back to you." She kept her voice as level as she could but didn't try to disguise her earnest supplication.

He didn't answer right away. If she asked what he suffered from, would he tell her? Likely not.

When he spoke, his voice sounded even wearier than before. "I know I would slow you down. I have been a burden to these." His gaze slid around the group. "I will go to my village. And I will pray for your success. I will grow strong to welcome you home with my wife. These others can ride with you."

A slight weight lifted from Meksem's chest, but uneasiness still churned in her belly. Surely he knew he couldn't make the journey back on his own. An able-bodied man would struggle with such a trip through the snow-covered mountains. As ill as Heinmot looked, he would never survive the hardships.

She glanced toward the two older warriors. Surely they would see reason.

But it was Alahmoot, Heinmot's younger brother, who spoke. "The boy can see him back. He is our sister's son. He will be a good help to my brother."

Would that be enough? Heinmot had traveled this far. Maybe with the lad along to take care of the horses, build fires, and do everything else they needed, the two could make it back to their village. Surely Heinmot's brother would not send him if it weren't safe.

Telípe would be devastated if something happened to her husband, but he was old enough to make his own choices.

As for the matter of these men riding with her and the others…

The sound of footsteps through the snow interrupted her thoughts, and Adam appeared through the darkness at the edge of the firelight.

She ignored the way her heart leapt at the sight of him, at the way his familiar gaze soaked over her, making sure she was well and safe among these strangers.

He glanced around the ring of men, then lowered himself to sit beside her. Sitting was a good move to show he trusted these new friends. But she could sense the wariness in him. She should tell him of the conversation so far, but maybe waiting until the others joined would be best.

She looked to Heinmot. "This is Adam." Should she say anything about him? That he was loyal, had proved himself strong in the face of pain, kind when treated coarsely, able to speak the language of the animals.

None of those traits would matter to these men, but every one had woven itself through her heart like roots of a seed coming to life. Proving him the best man she'd ever known.

Almost.

What would her father think of Adam? From what she could remember, the two of them had much in common. Both had the same way of looking deep inside her. Both had the same strength that could peel away into kindness just when she needed it most.

Her father would approve of Adam. Surely.

Maybe he would have even come to see Adam as the son he never had. If only...

More steps sounded as Caleb and French stepped into the light, Heinmot's nephew padding behind them. Then Susanna and Beaver Tail.

Meksem motioned for them all to sit, including Alahmoot, with the sweep of her hand. If he didn't trust them to sit in their presence, she wouldn't be joining her group with theirs.

Did it even make sense for them all to continue the journey together? Maybe. Riding as one band, they wouldn't be continually crossing each other's paths, confusing tracks from the other party with those of the Blackfoot band they sought.

As long as all could keep the pace she had to travel.

Susanna had carried the food pack near and began doling out baked camas root. Her actions seemed to loosen the tension in the air, especially when she handed food to the Salish men. Even Alahmoot took the root she offered him. Surely these men had supplies of their own, and Meksem would have to make sure they brought food if they worked out an agreement to travel together.

She'd gone to great effort to bring enough for those riding with her, and they carried a little extra since Elan had insisted Meksem not leave anything when she and Joel stayed behind. But Meksem wouldn't have enough to add three men to the party.

After she made introductions, both in Salish and the white men's tongue, silence settled over the group, interrupted only by the crackling of the fire and the occasional crunch of chewing. The food soothed the pinch in her belly, giving her strength for the conversation ahead.

When she finished her portion, she glanced at those who had

traveled with her. "Heinmot and this one"—she motioned toward the lad—"will go back to their village. I have given my word we will find the Blackfoot warriors and return Telípe to him."

Adam nodded, then flicked a glance at Alahmoot. Wondering about the other three men, no doubt.

Heinmot must have understood her words, for he spoke up in broken English. "My friends ride with you. Together... stronger in battle."

He might be right about that. The two older men looked trustworthy, but Alahmoot? Something about his manner didn't sit right with her. Maybe the feeling only came because he showed no respect for her as a warrior. Would he cause trouble among them? If he did, surely those with her would take her side.

She glanced at her friends again. Adam would stand by her, there was no doubt. He'd proved his loyalty more than once.

Caleb's large frame and solid expression bespoke his steadiness. He gave his friendship freely, and she had a feeling that his friendship, once given, would last for life.

French, with his easygoing manner and outrageous stories, possessed a shrewdness she'd sensed early on. She was fairly certain he would show the same loyalty Caleb offered.

Susanna's kindness seemed to know no end, yet the trait didn't make her gullible. More than once she'd proved herself tough when she needed to be.

And Beaver Tail. He'd won her respect—earning it with his keen abilities, his fair treatment and respect even for those who should be his enemies, and especially the caring way he loved Susanna.

But she could tell from only a single gaze between the two men that Alahmoot didn't feel the same respect for this Blackfoot brave that she did. She'd have to speak to Beaver Tail privately about doing his best to keep peace between them.

Probably he would do so without her saying anything. He seemed to value peace when possible.

Beaver Tail must have felt her gaze on him, for he glanced her way, his eyes speaking a message. The tiny nod of his chin made his thoughts clear. They should let these Salish men join with them. Sometimes, it was better to keep the unknowns closer where you could watch them.

She turned back to Heinmot and gave a solid nod. "They may ride with us." She'd chosen that wording specifically. *We will join with them* would have meant something entirely different, putting the power in the hands of men she didn't fully trust. "Eat and rest. We leave when the night is half through."

CHAPTER 11

*A*dam had slept with half his body awake, and now, as they rode through the darkness, the exhaustion weighing him down showed how little he'd rested.

He had to keep himself alert though, especially with the new members added to their group.

Before they'd parted from Heinmot, Meksem had questioned the man to learn everything he knew of the warriors who'd kidnapped the Salish women.

He knew little, it seemed. The captives were three women and a boy about five years old. They'd been taken, along with some horses, in the light of day while the women returned from tending their camas root fields.

At least the raiding party hadn't attacked the village. One woman had been with the others but escaped and returned to tell what had happened. She'd not been able to give any identifying markings, only to say there were seven Blackfoot warriors in the party.

Now, at least, they knew how many they were up against. And identifying the war party wouldn't be a problem. All they had to do was look for the captives.

He glanced behind him at Meksem, who'd taken her old place riding in the rear of the group. He'd planted himself right in front of her. Why he felt the need to protect her from the three new men, he wasn't certain yet.

A tiny part of him wondered if he worried more about her affections than her safety. The youngest of the three was about his own age, and Meksem's too, if he guessed correctly. Alahmoot was part of her people and clearly possessed strength and abilities she must admire. His face might be attractive too…at least he didn't have a hooked nose or beady eyes.

But Adam shouldn't be thinking that way. He couldn't deny his feelings for Meksem, but the last thing he should do was try to win her heart if she wished to give her affections to another. He craved her happiness even more than having her for himself.

Didn't he? He *wanted* her happiness to be his goal. But maybe he wasn't noble enough.

Tar and feathers. Just when he'd found some focus about Meksem, with his determination to win her affections. Maybe meeting this stranger was God's way of telling him to fix his attention on their mission, not on winning the strong woman's heart.

At last, dawn broke across the eastern horizon, proving Beaver Tail had kept them moving in a northeasterly direction. He pushed them hard, as hard as the horses could manage without wearing them down too much. Good thing Beaver didn't ride one of the spotted horses, for if he was used to their stamina, he might ask more than the other animals could manage.

When they moved onto a section of the trail wide enough for two abreast, he motioned for Meksem to come up alongside him.

When she did, he nodded toward her horse. "How is it the Palouse horses have so much more stamina than the others?

What do your people breed into them? The farther we go, the more difference I see in them."

She tipped her head and pinched her mouth in a thoughtful pose. "I know not where the first ones came from. We only breed the strongest horses to continue the line. We ask much of them but care much for them too."

He couldn't help a tired grin. "That sentiment I completely agree with."

She gave a single nod. "I learned early to judge a man by the way he treats his animals." Something in that statement felt like a compliment, but maybe she didn't mean him specifically.

She saved him a response when she slid a glance to Tesoro, who walked on his tether line with his head near Adam's stirrup. "Not all are as spirited as that one."

Adam stroked the gelding's forelock, and the animal rubbed its head against his leg. "He's learning to trust me. His strong spirit only means I have to take my time with him." He sent her a sideways look. "A fact he reminded me of yesterday morning."

Her gaze softened and flicked down his back. "You still feel pain?"

"Not much. Am I doing better about hiding it?" He kept his tone light.

The corners of her mouth twitched. "Better."

～

Meksem kept watch over the new men carefully throughout the day. Ukugnut and Yaka, the two older braves, both seemed to possess the wisdom and rational minds that came with age. Alahmoot stayed quiet, keeping to himself. Her nerves loosened around them as the hours wore on.

Caleb, of course, welcomed the newcomers with his usual friendly manner. The difference in language didn't seem to bother him. He simply used what little sign language he knew, that common method all the tribes used to communicate. In the past, she'd wondered if white men used the same gestures, but from the little these men knew, the signs must only be used among the tribes.

Several times throughout the day, one of the others would motion her forward to act as translator. The benefit of being the only person able to speak both Salish and the white tongue came in the fact that she always knew what was happening.

Overhead, the sky grew darker as the sun sank lower in the west. The clouds spoke of snow, but the first moisture to fall dropped wet and heavy on Meksem's nose.

Not rain. Snow would be bad enough, but rain would soak through any opening in their buckskins. With the frigid air around them, they'd be coated in ice before long.

Ahead of her, faces rose to the sky as the others felt the drops too. Would they want to take shelter? A line of trees ran alongside their path, which could provide cover, especially if they draped furs between the branches. But that would mean a delay of precious time. Even if the Blackfoot party also had to stop and take refuge from the weather, they had a head start.

Beaver Tail kept riding. A new flood of thankfulness washed through her for the man. He possessed gumption, she couldn't deny it.

As more rain fell in large drops, spattering in a steady sprinkle, no one turned to question her. Adam did look back once to send her a wry smile. She returned the expression with a look hopefully more determined than grim. He felt her worry—she could see it in the grooves across his brow. But at least none of them asked to stop.

As the rainfall grew heavier, bits of ice mixed in with the water. She pulled her coat tighter around her, tucking herself like a turtle as deep in the fur as she could.

The horses would get the brunt of the cold, but at least

moving would help keep them warm. Onward they rode, but the thick clouds kept her from knowing how long they traveled with icy pellets raining down on them.

Ahead, Beaver Tail called the signal to halt, and she strained to see what made him stop. As far as she could tell, there wasn't a level spot here suitable for them to rest. Perhaps he could see something she didn't. As wet and frozen as they all were, maybe the time had come to take shelter and try to nurture a warming fire. Her cold-numbed limbs ached at the thought.

Beaver dismounted and handed his reins to Susanna.

Just in front of Meksem, Adam craned his neck to see, as well. Then he turned to look back at her, hope brightening his face. "I think it's a cave. Beaver just went inside."

A surge of excitement slipped through her. Would the space within be large enough for them all to take shelter? The horses too?

The latter wasn't likely. She'd seen a few caves when she traveled with hunting parties or explored the mountains on her own. Most were shallow, sometimes not more than indentations in the rock. A few had been deeper, winding far into the mountainside. But they often sloped steeply downward, and sometimes they held creatures or dank smells that would keep the horses from venturing in.

Beaver Tail was wise to go in first to investigate. She couldn't help remembering back to the first time she'd met him, a memory that brought a smile now, although she'd been angry as a wet mountain lion at the time. She and Elan had taken shelter from a winter storm much like this one in a cave on the Lolo Trail. Beaver Tail's group had been traveling the other direction at the time, searching for Adam.

Beaver had come into that cave to scout it, much like he was doing now. Somehow, he'd sensed her and Elan hiding in the darkness. He'd known exactly where she was, proving himself a better warrior. With a single charge, he'd won the upper hand, then marched them out into the daylight. She could still feel a twinge of bitterness in her chest at such sound defeat, but he'd not hurt them.

Actually, Joel and the others had offered her and Elan food. While waiting out the storm in that cave, Joel had spoken of their search for his brother and eventually talked the two of them into serving as guides back through the mountains. Helping with their search to find Adam.

If she'd known at the time exactly who Adam was—how much he would affect her—would she have been more eager to find him...or less?

When this journey ended and they parted ways, how hard would it be to see him ride away?

Or did he plan to leave? Now that his brother would be married to Elan, maybe he'd stay in the Nimiipuu camp too. Did she want that? So much uncertainty churned inside her.

"There he is." Adam's voice warmed with excitement.

She nudged Apash up closer to Adam's geldings and glimpsed Beaver Tail as he collected his reins from Susanna. He sent a glance over the group. "There's room inside for us to eat and build a fire. For the horses too, at least some of them. Need light to see for sure."

His words sent a rush of relief through her just as a shiver shook her frame. They did need to rest. Getting warm would give them strength to endure another stretch of riding.

The group dismounted, though there wasn't much room to move along the thin trail edging the side of the mountain. Inside the cave, Beaver Tail and Susanna built a fire while the rest of them brought in a few needed supplies. It wouldn't be safe to lead the horses in until they had a better feel for the layout. Surely none of the animals would step inside, as dark as it was.

When Beaver finally lit a spark that flamed to life on the tinder, she scanned the round cavern. They could probably fit all the animals, or most of them.

"I'll start bringing in horses." She stepped into the still-falling ice and snow.

They tried Susanna's gelding first, but the animal balked at the dark opening and refused to step inside. Maybe the dim interior hindered him, or the smell of whatever animals had taken shelter there in the past, or maybe the smoke sifting out of the opening.

"Let me try my mare." She handed the gelding's reins to French. "Apash has come into many caves." She and the mare had spent time in tighter spaces than this one. If Meksem led her, Apash probably wouldn't blink an eye.

Getting her past the other horses on the trail proved the hardest part, but once they reached the cave opening, Apash stepped inside without complaint.

"Good, girl." She patted the mare's neck, then handed her reins to Susanna and stepped back out for the next horse.

One by one they managed to pack nine of the twelve horses into the cave. Adam tried several times to lead his spotted gelding into the shelter, but the animal planted its feet and refused. After three attempts, he stopped trying, for it became clear the last three horses wouldn't fit anyway. His two geldings and Yaka's horse were left outside.

The weight of Adam's worry clouded his eyes as he stroked his animals. She stepped toward him, her chest heavy as she joined him beside the spotted gelding. Rain splashed on her nose as she rubbed the slick hair on the animal's neck. "He is no stranger to snow." The comment was such a paltry encouragement, but she knew no other words to ease Adam's worry.

He seemed to understand what she wasn't able to express, for when he looked over at her, his gaze held a thank-you that was clear even through the falling snow.

With a nod and a sigh, he turned away from the horse. "I've done everything I can for them. Let's get inside to the fire."

Bodies crowded the cave as they all crouched around the

flame, and the stink of wet horseflesh mixed with the thick wood smoke. With so much warmth cloying the place, their clothing would be dry quickly. Adam rose twice while they ate, stepping to the cave entrance to peer out at his horses.

The second time, she joined him there. A fierce wind whipped the snow outside, making the view hazy, especially with the darkness that had settled. The warm calm of the cave made the fighting fury of the snowstorm outside feel like a different world. Thankfully, Adam didn't step into the blizzard, only leaned out far enough to see all three horses down the trail.

When they both pulled back in the cave, he glanced at her, a furrow lining his brow. "I hate to leave them."

"Our people have bred this spotted horse to survive winters like these. He is strong. These others will manage too."

His throat worked and he nodded, but uncertainty still shone in his eyes.

She reached up and laid a hand on his upper arm, an action she would never have done before. But…this seemed right.

The touch accomplished the comfort her words hadn't. Some of the worry faded from his expression as he searched her eyes. His gaze drove deep, seeing all the way to her core.

He laid his hand over hers, then took her fingers in his, removing her hand from his arm and holding it with both of his. His gaze never left her eyes, but his expression turned searching. As though looking for something inside her he hadn't yet found.

Heat crept up her neck, and her instinct was to pull her hand from his.

But she didn't. Not yet.

Were the others watching them? With their backs facing the group, no one should be able to see their hands. What did Adam mean by the touch?

He didn't say anything, just held her hand in both of his, one thumb stroking the back in a gentle caress.

The movement spread warmth all the way up her arm. She'd so rarely been touched, even as a girl. And no contact had ever flowed all the way through her the way his did. She wasn't sure she could pull her hand back if she wanted to.

At last, he gave a final stroke, then released her. "Guess we better sleep while we can."

He turned back to the fire, but she stayed where she was. In truth, she needed a few moments to gather her wits about her. As much as she hated not being in firm control of herself, the pleasure in Adam's touch almost made up for the struggle.

More than made up for it.

She checked each of the horses in the cave, making sure they were tied securely to rocks heavy enough to keep them still, making sure girths were loose so the animals could rest. When she finished, her body had finally settled enough for her to move back to her place at the fire.

As she eased into her seat beside Adam, she took care not to look his way. If she had a good reason for asking one of the others to switch places with her, she might have moved to a different seat. But most of the group had already bedded down, feet to the fire and heads fanning away like rays of the sun from its center.

She settled into her furs but had to lie on her back so she wasn't facing Adam on one side or Susanna snuggled into Beaver Tail on the other.

As she stared up at the cave's high ceiling, the flickering flames dancing off the dark stone, loneliness settled in her chest. This ache had been her companion more times than she could count through the years, but with all these people crowded around her, the intensity of the pain raised the sting of tears to her eyes. She pressed her lids shut, locking in the moisture.

What more did she need from life? She'd worked hard to

earn her position among the warriors. Even now she led this unlikely group to win back her sister and the other captives.

She should feel strong and courageous, not so lonely her entire body ached. The longing inside yearned as though she'd not yet found a part of herself. The part that brought her fulfillment. Was it a man she craved? The man beside her?

His touch did warm her in ways no one else ever had.

But something more she was missing. A purpose she'd been created for. Maybe, if she sought hard enough, she would finally find that missing piece.

CHAPTER 12

*A*dam woke to a stillness that needled all the way through his chest.

He lay quietly for a moment, taking in the deep breathing of those all around him. Warmth spread through the cave, even though the fire had died to ashes. A chewing sound drifted from one of the horses, a stomp from another.

His heart lurched. What of the animals outside? The quiet must mean the storm had passed.

He eased himself up, doing his best not to wake any of the others. A glance toward the entrance showed a dim light, either moonlight shimmering off the white snow, or dawn just now breaking. That light in the mountain sky usually brought a sense of hope, but he couldn't shake the dread seeping through his chest.

Like the others, he'd slept in his boots and coat, so he grabbed his gloves and started toward the cave opening. As he slipped his fingers into the buckskin, he couldn't help remembering how he'd held Meksem's hand in his. Her fingers had been strong, her hand chapped from the icy wind.

And so capable.

From the look in her eyes, his touch had startled her as much as it had him. The contact had affected her.

The time had come to face the truth. He'd fallen hard for this woman, and he didn't want to get over her. He would do whatever it took to make her feel the same.

He poked his head outside first, his eyes searching out the three horses waiting patiently on the trail.

Yaka's gelding stood with its head drooped in a doze, a layer of snow coating its long winter hair. Adam's riding horse stood behind, tail rustling in the breeze. Where was Tesoro?

Fear snaked through his chest as he stepped into the cold. The young gelding might have moved off the trail, standing down on the slope where the other horses blocked his view.

But as Adam moved down the path, the fear spread to his belly, turning into a knot of bile.

Tesoro was gone.

He slid past the two geldings and out onto the open trail behind them. "Tesoro?"

The gelding wouldn't know his name yet but might recognize Adam's voice. If he would just nicker, or even paw the snow, maybe the sound would show him where to look.

He scanned the white mountains around them. The only dark spots were trees capped with ice and snow that made them look like mushrooms. He dropped his gaze to the ground where the horse had stood. Snow covered the tracks, making them look like dips in the ice. He peered closer hoping to find a trail showing which way the horse had gone.

Nothing.

As he raised his gaze back to the landscape around him, desperation swelled in his chest. Cupping his hands around his mouth, he yelled, "Tesoro!" His cry echoed across the still mountains, the slight wind not stealing the word as the rocks pitched the sound back at him.

Such an enormous expanse stretched around him. And somewhere in the midst of it all, his special horse wandered.

He should have found a way to bring the animal in the cave. The horse had already proved his disregard for restraint when he panicked. The thin rope that tied him to a rock outside couldn't have kept the animal in place when fear struck.

"Adam?"

He spun, his eyes half expecting to see Meksem holding the spotted gelding's lead line.

But she stood alone by the cave's entrance. She pulled her hood up over her long black braid, but her face still wore that sleep-rumpled look. Seeing her like that always tightened his belly, making him want to reach out and pull her into his arms.

But this time, not even that sensation could push aside the fear churning in him.

"He's gone. My treasure, he's gone." The panic in his tone reflected the emotion welling inside him.

Pain slipped over Meksem's face, and she strode toward him, running her hand along both horses as she passed them. When she reached Adam, her gaze dropped to the snow-covered tracks at his feet, and her brow furrowed as she studied them.

"I can't tell which way he went. Can you?" He should go wake Beaver Tail and French. Both men had honed their tracking skills.

Then he would saddle his riding horse. If the others couldn't find which way Tesoro had gone, he'd start by backtracking the trail they'd traveled the day before. Maybe the horse had followed the familiar path.

Of course, Tesoro had proved that, when he panicked, he lost all regard for rational actions.

"I think these are his tracks." Meksem had walked a few paces back down the trail. She straightened and turned to him. "Let's pack up. We'll all look for him."

Adam shook his head as he turned and started scraping the

snow crust from his riding horse's back. "We don't all need to go. Surely he hasn't gone far." And having so many people along would slow him down. He had to ride hard. Tesoro must have taken off while the snowstorm was still raging, so who knew how far he'd gone?

Meksem didn't answer but made her way past him into the cave. When he went in for his saddle, she was telling the others what happened, first in English, then in Salish. The young brave, Alahmoot, spoke something back to her in a measured tone, but Adam couldn't understand the language. He would learn it in time, but this certainly wasn't that moment.

As he finished saddling his gelding, Meksem led her mare out of the cave.

A wave of frustration slid through him. He didn't mind her coming, but any more than her would slow him down. "Is it just you?"

"Yes." She led her mare down the slope to get around the horses standing on the narrow trail. Beaver Tail, Caleb, and French stepped out of the cave and stood on the path to watch.

He swung aboard his mount and glanced at them. "We'll be back when we find him." Surely, if they moved quickly, they'd locate the horse and be back in a few hours. He couldn't think past that.

"We'll be praying." Caleb's voice rang deep, penetrating his focus.

If the Almighty would hear Caleb's prayer, so much the better. They needed all the help they could get to find one lone horse in this massive wilderness.

Adam could only nod his thanks. The lump in his throat stopped any words. Then, with a glance to make sure Meksem was ready, he nudged his horse back down the trail.

The farther they rode, the more thankful he was to have Meksem with him. She possessed a keen eye, and he would have missed the place where Tesoro turned off the main trail to take cover in a small grove of trees. Snow coated his tracks, making them look like small valleys in the ice.

But once he rode into the woods, the prints became much easier to spot.

The horse had ambled through the cluster of trees, eating bark from some and leaving behind barren patches in the trunks. Meksem had been the first to spot these too.

When his belly gave a loud rumble, she reached into the pack behind her saddle and pulled out a chunk of roasted elk meat. "Susanna sent this for us." She held out a piece larger than what they normally allotted themselves in a single meal.

He took the meat, tore it in half, then handed one part back to her.

She shook her head. "You eat. I am not hungry."

Not true, surely. Neither of them had taken time to break their fast before leaving the cave. This was probably the only food she brought.

He extended the meat toward her again. "Eat." He didn't mean his voice to sound so gruff, but the worry churning inside him made it hard to keep a rein on himself.

She took the food and bit off a chunk, not meeting his gaze.

He straightened and turned his focus back to the woods around them. "Have you found which direction he went when he left these trees?"

She nudged her mare forward, riding toward the southwest corner of the woods. "I saw tracks leading out over here."

Sending Meksem must have been God's way of looking out for him. A twinge shot through Adam's chest. Maybe letting Caleb pray wasn't enough. Perhaps he should request the Almighty's help in finding Tesoro too.

Almighty God, I don't know the right words to ask. But please bring back my horse. Take us to him. Let him be safe.

From what he'd learned, most of the animals that would prey on a horse were either hibernating from the cold or didn't often venture this deep into the mountains. Although a mountain lion might expand its hunting area if game was scarce.

But the treacherous landscape worried him more than anything. The horse had left the trail, and anything could happen traveling over these icy rocks.

A horse could slip on a patch of ice and go down. These slopes were steep enough that a stumble could easily turn into a roll down an embankment. Or over a cliff...

He pushed the thoughts aside as they left the shelter of the trees. Meksem was right about the tracks being Tesoro's. The horse must've waited till the snowfall ended before leaving shelter, for the prints looked fresh and mostly unmarred.

Meksem pushed her mare into a trot up the hill, and he followed, though fire shot through his hip and back with every stride. A searing reminder of the fall he'd taken just two days before. Would that be the only time he ever rode Tesoro?

The horse had traveled in a haphazard rhythm, first lunging straight up a mountain slope, then cutting downward, then moving around the side as it clambered over snow-covered rocks. From the angle and spread of the hoof prints, Tesoro must have been traveling at a brisk trot. Several times, long streaks showed how the horse had slid over ice. Adam's gut twisted at one area where the snow was churned more than the others. He must have fallen here. If Tesoro didn't slow down, he would do real damage to himself.

Adam's priceless treasure. If he fell and broke a limb, what could be done to save him? There would be no choice but to put the animal out of his misery. But he wasn't sure he could bring himself... And how could he face Meksem if he lost the special gift she'd sacrificed to give him?

He nudged his mount faster, but a shadow in the snow grabbed his attention. As he leaned forward for a better angle, recognition brought the taste of bile up his throat.

Blood.

Meksem saw it too and pressed her mouth in a grim line.

He scrambled for an explanation that wouldn't assume the worst. "Maybe it's just a little cut. He nicked himself on the edge of the rock. Maybe the injury will slow him down." There was a hopeful thought.

She only nodded as she nudged her mare forward.

Following Tesoro's trail without endangering their mounts proved a challenge, but at least the horse's prints proved easy to see in the fresh snow. Somehow, he'd managed to crisscross the sides of two mountains during the morning hours they tracked him. The sun had risen almost to the center of the sky, warming the air and shimmering off snow with a blinding light.

His eyes had formed a permanent squint, the lines on his face embedding deeply as he fought to see enough through the brilliant rays to follow the tracks.

The one thing he couldn't miss as they traveled were the splashes of red dotting the snow around many of the hoof prints. Tesoro still bled.

Where was he injured? And why hadn't they at least caught sight of the gelding ahead of them? How much time would they lose in their hunt for the Blackfoot because of this thick-headed horse?

Meksem must be steaming inside, but she didn't let it show. Never once did she reveal any frustration during their search, only intense focus as she shifted her gaze between the tracks and the path ahead.

She served mostly as their guide, maneuvering the rocks and cliffs and steep slopes ahead of him while he examined the tracks they passed, watching for any signs of change. Of course, he also kept a steady scanning of the distant landscape for the spotted gelding.

As they rounded a large boulder—a rock that looked famil-iar, but then, every part of these mountains had begun to look the same—a new set of tracks caught his eye.

Smaller, in the shape of a dog or cat. A large cat.

He reined in his mount. "Look."

Meksem spun to see where he pointed, halting her horse midstride. After peering for only a heartbeat at the tracks, her face tightened into an angry mask. "Mountain cat." She stared up at the incline on their right, scanning each crag with a calculating gaze.

The words sent a flash flood of fear through him. He kicked his gelding forward. "We have to get him."

His blood pounded hard through his chest as he pushed his mount faster than he should over the icy rocks. He pulled out his rifle and readied the bullet.

The mountain lion had a lead on them, surely drawn by the blood from Tesoro's wound. Could the cat travel faster than their horses over this terrain? Probably.

Maybe he could still get there in time to save the horse's life.

As they rounded the curve of the mountainside, a dark spot in the distance twisted his gut.

Tesoro.

CHAPTER 13

*E*ven as Adam kicked his mount harder, he strained to see the details of the horse. Was he standing? No.

Or maybe… Maybe he was standing in a low spot behind a rock. The animal's head hung low, a position that didn't look possible were he lying on his side.

And where was the cougar? No sign of him that Adam could see.

He'd covered half the distance since he first saw the horse, and Tesoro had surely noticed them approaching. Adam could just see the flicking of an ear, although the horse didn't raise its head.

God, if you're listening. Help him. Don't let me lose him. Please.

As he drew near, he shifted his reins to raise the rifle into firing position. If Tesoro still stood, the mountain lion must not have attacked him yet. The predator might be crouching nearby.

Meksem rode just behind Adam, and when she gasped, he focused hard on the horse to see what she'd seen. A light brown lump lay just beyond the spotted horse. Adam's heart pulsed even harder. Could it be? Stretched out the way it was, the cougar looked to be half the size of the large gelding…and dead.

Very dead.

Adam kept a grip on his gun as he reined his horse to a stop just before Tesoro. He gave the cat a final glance to make sure it didn't move, then turned his full focus on his treasured animal.

Tesoro stood with his left front hoof cocked, not bearing any weight on the leg. He kept his head lowered in a miserable pose.

Adam approached slowly, taking in the shredded skin blending with the dark hair of his chest. Powerful claws had scraped through the hide, and blood ran down his front legs. Adam reached out and stroked the gelding's forehead. "Hey, boy."

The horse gave a soft nicker of greeting, a sound that formed a lump in Adam's throat.

"I'm sorry, fella. I tried to get here in time." He slid his gaze to the cat lying only a couple strides away. Crimson marred the tan fur on its face and front paws.

Tesoro's blood, no doubt.

But the mangled fur and bloodied gashes on its belly must have been damage inflicted by the horse.

Relief rose up in his chest and he rubbed the horse's head again. "You did well."

Meksem stepped around him to investigate the gelding's other side, and Adam turned his attention there too. The hoof he favored was drenched in blood, but most of the crimson looked to be dripping from the wounds on the horse's chest.

Meksem crouched beside the leg and pointed to a band of white flesh peeking through the red. "Teeth marks here." She scooped snow in her gloved hands and pressed it gently to the area, then used more snow to wipe the bloody ice away.

The mangled skin showed clearly now and did look like teeth marks. Maybe the cat's desperate attempt to stop hooves from pounding into its flesh.

Adam stroked the gelding's shoulder as he scanned the rest

of the horse's body. He moved behind, then around to the other side.

A few cuts and places where the hair had been scraped off, but the worst damage seem to be on Tesoro's chest and that left front leg.

Meksem now crouched at the horse's chest. "It's so cold, the blood is frozen. That might have saved his life."

Adam bent beside her and pulled off a glove to feel the liquid. Ice crystals glittered in some spots, and Meksem was right that a crust of ice had formed over much of the blood.

A surge of gratitude washed through him. A miracle. This had to be a miracle. *Thank You, God.*

He stood and stroked the horse's neck, studying his drooping head. "He's lost a lot of blood. He'll pull out of it though. Don't you think?"

Meksem stood beside him.

For a long moment, the two of them rubbed the horse in silence. If gentle hands and affection could cure an animal, this one would spring to full vigor any minute.

Tesoro did lift his head a little.

Adam moved his hand to let the horse sniff in their usual greeting. "We have a long way to go back, boy. Think you can make it?" Just the thought of how hard it would be—how painful—for the horse to walk the distance back to the cave, tightened a knot in his belly.

But that would be only a minor trek compared to the span they had to travel to catch up with the Blackfoot band. They'd lost so much time today. He should have found a better way to secure Tesoro, maybe another shelter for him since the animal wouldn't enter the cave. Had his negligence in caring for Tesoro caused such a delay that they wouldn't be able to catch up with the kidnappers?

God in heaven, You kept him safe. Kept him alive, just as I prayed.

Now, Almighty God, don't let my carelessness make us fail in this mission to save Meksem's sister. Please.

~

small part of Meksem wanted to scream with frustration about the day's delay this horse had caused. But the other part of her—the much bigger part—wanted to wrap her arms around Adam.

She knew better than anyone how much the animal meant to him—what tender care he showed toward all animals. And seeing this troublesome gelding in so much pain, an animal that had stolen his heart, had to be tying his middle in knots.

He turned to her and seemed to be gathering himself for the next step. "Can you lead my mount? I'm going to walk Tesoro. Go on ahead. We'll need to take it slowly."

She shook her head. There was no way she would leave him alone out here.

He spoke again before she could answer. "Should we take the wildcat carcass with us? There hasn't been much hunting in these mountains, and I'm sure we could use the meat."

A plan formed in her mind with his words, one she should have thought of already. "Start walking back to the cave with Tesoro. I'll cut out the meat, then catch up with you." She would reach him long before he covered half of their back trail.

Uncertainty flicked across his face, but then he nodded. "All right."

She watched as Adam tugged the horse into its first step. The animal jerked in a heavy limp, putting only a tiny bit of weight on the wounded leg. But the next step seemed easier, and the third better still.

Wrapping the injuries in snow would help numb the pain and keep them from swelling, but packed snow would be hard to hold in place while the horse walked. Better to wait until they reached the cave. Or, if they had to, they could stop a few times along the way to hold ice to the wounds.

After the horse had taken a handful of steps, Adam glanced back at her. The weary half-smile he sent her spread a warm ache through her chest. As much as she hated to see the horse injured, she hated even more the pain Tesoro's wounds brought to Adam.

When he faced forward again, she turned to her work with the wildcat. The sooner she finished this task, the sooner she could rejoin Adam. There wasn't much she could do to ease his pain, but her heart told her being with him would help more than anything. She just couldn't be certain if the time together was for her benefit, or for his.

And that was a question she wasn't ready to face yet.

～

The afternoon stretched long before them as Meksem strolled beside Adam. They walked on a game trail etched into the side of a gentle slope, near enough their original tracks she could make sure they didn't veer off course.

"Did they ever tell you how I got separated from Joel and the others?" Adam had been talkative through the afternoon, telling stories of his journey across the great water with his brother, then how they met each of the other men along the way to her people's land.

The three horses ambled behind them, the spotted gelding keeping a steady pace with much less limp than he'd started out with.

She glanced sideways at Adam. "No. I wondered."

Walking beside him gave her the perfect view of his strong profile. The way each of his features rested perfectly in his face, each line carved by a master, not wasting any space. His dark lashes were longer than any man's she'd seen, and when he talked, a dimple pressed into his cheek. Did the other side dimple, as well?

He looked at her, his arresting eyes catching her staring. She tried to drop her gaze, but one look in those eyes, and she was locked in place.

A smile crept up the sides of his cheeks. There was that dimple, and no, the other side didn't press as this one did. Maybe that was only because his teasing grin tipped more on one side than the other.

She bit her lip as heat crawled onto her face. She shouldn't stare at him so. What must he think of it? Did he realize the way his gaze caught her breath, warming her all the way through? Or the way his nearness made her middle flutter?

The way she lost a little control of herself didn't bother her as much as it used to. Somehow, she felt safe with him. If she relinquished control into his hands, he would ensure she was protected. She didn't have to work to earn his respect. He gave it freely.

Finally, he released his hold on her gaze, turning to the path ahead. "We'd been traveling up the Missouri River—Joel, Caleb, and I. French had joined up with us too. We met a Mandan chief on the way up the river who told us about the unusual horses of the Shoshone and Nez Perce. I really wanted to see them. Horses have always been a weakness of mine."

He sent her a pained grin. "A couple of braves were taking a more direct route to trade with the Shoshone, and they invited me to ride with them. To see the great horses the Mandan spoke of with spots all over their bodies and superior abilities in speed and endurance."

He paused to inhale a breath, as though gathering strength to go on. "Joel didn't want to change our plans. Winter was coming fast, and we were pushing hard to reach Beaver Tail's camp before the snow grew bad." His voice turned emotionless. "I snuck out one night, leaving a note for Joel saying I was going with those two braves. We'd winter with their people and find the horses the Mandan told us about. When spring came, I'd follow the Missouri north to catch up with them at Beaver Tail's camp."

A silence settled over them except for the swishing of footsteps in snow. The weight of Adam's sorrow hung heavily in the air.

When he spoke again, his voice had lost its edge. "I shouldn't have left. I knew it even then. I just didn't want to make Joel feel guilty for holding me back, and I didn't want to drag him with me against his will." He sent a wry grin her way. "My brother's always felt like he had to look out for me, ever since that stallion stomped me when I was a boy."

She scanned her memory for the horse he meant. He'd once mentioned another horse he loved, one with a spirit like Tesoro's. "Fritz?"

Surprise slipped through his eyes, and he nodded. "Fritz was a handful. He'd been taught to ride before my father purchased him, but none of our lads would get near him. He'd charge the fence with teeth bared. But he was so majestic and had this look in his eye… I knew if I could gain his trust, we could become good friends." He slid another look her way. "The bet I made with one of our stable hands had nothing to do with it, that was just a way to make sure I didn't let my nerves get the better of me."

She could well imagine a lad with Adam's rich black hair, his orange eyes turning dreamy as he perched with his arms crossed on the fence, watching a magnificent stallion prance.

Then his other words slipped in to taint the image. "He hurt you?" Even though she knew how the story ended, pain still tightened in her chest at the thought of him in danger.

Adam scrunched his nose. "He was coming along so well. We'd been doing groundwork for several weeks. He never bit at me anymore, and he'd become quite affectionate actually. I thought he was ready for a saddle. Turned out I was rushing things."

She had to fight back a grin, even though the story wasn't funny. Nor was the reminder of his fall from Tesoro. But the similarities between the two experiences glared sharply in her mind.

He let out a sigh. "I know. Haven't quite learned that lesson, have I?" Then a warm chuckle slipped from him, forming a white cloud in front of his mouth. "Maybe I have now though." He paused, and turned back to rub the spotted gelding's face. "Maybe this is a turning point for him, like when Fritz stomped me halfway to eternity."

He turned back to the trail again and started walking. "Anyway, Joel stayed by my side for weeks while I recovered. The doctor told my parents I wouldn't make it, and I think they gave up on me at that point. But Joel never did." His voice turned soft, almost wistful. "All these years he's never given up on me."

Her chest squeezed. Elan had been that way with her. She'd accepted Meksem when they first met as young girls, even though Meksem had always tagged along with the boys when the youths had split out in different games. Elan's patience never wore thin, even when Meksem didn't open up the way she knew her friend wanted. Even when Meksem pulled away, not able to bring herself to respond when her friend reached out. Somehow, Elan seemed to know when Meksem needed her, and she was there—always there—somehow knowing just what would help.

Adam spoke again, pulling her from the memories. "I guess that's why I thought it would be best to sneak away with those Mandan braves while Joel and the others slept. I wanted him to have a chance to find his own adventures." Another chuckle drifted out. "I guess he did at that. He might never have met Elan if he and the others hadn't been out chasing after me."

Then he turned those orange eyes on her. "And I might never have met you."

The awareness sparking between them pressed the breath from her chest. Was he saying she meant to him what Elan meant to Joel? Those two were to be married...might be married already. Surely Adam didn't mean he cared that much for her.

She had to say something to break the thickness humming through the air.

But Adam beat her to it. He shifted back to the trail ahead of them, and his voice turned jesting. "And we might not be traipsing through the snow-covered mountains together, dragging an injured horse who delayed us a day in the hunt for your sister."

His face scrunched in a look of distaste. "I'm sorry, Meksem. I really am." He glanced sideways with apology in his eyes. "I don't know what to do now that he's injured. Maybe it's best you all ride ahead. I'll let him rest a little, then follow you at a pace he can manage."

At least he'd opened the conversation that had hung as a silent weight around her neck—probably around his too. Although, his suggestion settled in her gut like foul-tasting fish.

She shook her head. "We stay together." Weren't those the same words he'd spoken to her not long after they entered the mountains, when she'd wanted to send the rest of the group back? Now, the positions had switched, but the outcome would stay the same.

She wasn't leaving this man behind to face the struggles in this snowy wilderness on his own. And in truth, she didn't want to face what lay ahead without him either. Did that make her weak?

CHAPTER 14

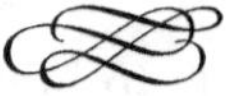

They had to make a plan.

Meksem glanced back at the spotted gelding, who plodded along steadily. He still limped, but not as much as she would have expected. "When we get to the cave, we wrap ice on the wounds. Then rest a while." Darkness would have fallen by then. "After that, we all ride together. When he needs to stop, we stop." That would have to do.

But what of Telípe? Would this decision mean the difference between life and death for her sister? For the young babe growing within her?

Maybe Meksem and a few of the others should ride ahead. Adam could go slower with the rest of the group. Would that be best? Her mind said that plan made sense.

So what stopped her? Every time she thought of leaving Adam, even with capable companions, fear clutched tight around her throat.

Simply because she wouldn't be here to help him? To keep him safe? Adam was as capable as she was, maybe more so, depending on the threat. She hated being out of control, espe-cially when it came to something—or someone—important to her. But maybe this was a situation where she would have to trust others.

Still, her belly churned at the thought of leaving him. Could the caution be a greater power warning her? She'd never put stock in the Great Spirit the shaman spoke of. She'd never seen evidence of his existence, or at least that he played any part in The People's lives. She wasn't sure about the white man's God either. Did Adam believe in him?

That was a question she'd not considered before. Wouldn't all white men follow their God? But that would be like assuming that just because she was one of The People, she believed in all the beings the shamans spoke of. She glanced sideways at him. "Do you follow the God of the white man?"

He met her gaze, brows raised. "I...do." His face took on an odd expression. "More so now than I did this morning."

She tipped her head, trying to make sense of his words. "You didn't follow Him this morning?"

A half-smile touched his mouth. Not as if he was making fun of her. No, this was a smile that bespoke wonder. "I've been taught about Him all my life. But I guess I always thought He was too distant to care much." He raised a shoulder. "At least to care about me. I never was very pious."

She struggled to decipher both his words and the deeper meaning of what he was saying. For some reason, his thoughts on his God mattered to her more than she would have expected.

"This morning when we were hunting Tesoro," he continued, "there were so many times I wondered how we would find him in this massive wilderness. Then, when we saw that the wildcat was tracking him, I knew there was no way we would reach him in time."

He shrugged again, but the motion did nothing to steal the importance from his words. "I prayed. I asked God to save him. And...it looks like He did." Adam glanced back at the horse, and his mouth tipped in a grin that lit his face. "Against all odds."

A few beats of silence settled as Meksem turned the words over in her mind, then Adam spoke again, his voice warm and deep. "Just now, I prayed that we wouldn't be too late for Telípe. That we would still catch up to the Blackfoot and get her and the others safely away."

His words slipped through her, leaving an unsettled feeling in her chest. Had his God answered his prayer about the horse? Would He answer his prayer about Telípe? What would it be like to have such a powerful God Who cared enough to bother Himself with the needs of individual people?

If only she could have such a God for herself.

~

*A*dam stared at the tender flesh exposed on Tesoro's chest.

Finally, they'd made it back to the cave. The gelding had been so weary and in such pain by the time they arrived that he'd allowed himself to be led inside the cavern. Between Susanna and Meksem, they'd cleaned the wounds thoroughly, allowing a clear view of the true extent of the injuries.

The claws that scraped his chest had peeled away thick layers of flesh, revealing muscle and tissue beneath. Walking for so long had swollen the injured areas, but loss of blood was probably the worst damage. That's what would have killed the horse.

The blood freezing on the wound had probably saved Tesoro's life. A miracle only God could've accomplished.

"Let's see if we can get this tied around his chest." French stepped beside Adam and pressed a cloth-wrapped bundle to the horse's front. "You hold it there, and I'll tie it around his neck and legs."

Within minutes, French stepped back to admire his work. The wrap wasn't bad considering what few materials they had to work with. "That should hold while he's standing still. We'll just keep filling it with snow when what's in there melts."

Adam pushed up to his feet and stepped away from the horse. "Rest now, boy. You'll feel better soon."

French laid a hand on Adam's shoulder. "You and Meksem need to sleep too. We all do. You think we'll start riding again at first light?"

Adam shook his head. "We just need a few hours' sleep, then we can ride out a little after midnight like we usually do." His middle still churned at the thought that he and Tesoro would slow the group down—even more than they'd already done. And if the pace Meksem needed to travel proved too much for the gelding, he might have to insist the others go on without him. That thought of Meksem facing the dangers of a war party without him there to help settled like kerosene poured in a fire, but he might have no other choice. They'd have to take things one step at a time.

Sleep would be the first goal. His exhausted body was threatening to keel over right where he stood. Too many nights with too little sleep.

~

The mountains were beginning to change.

Meksem had been so weary as daylight broke in the eastern sky, she'd not noticed how much larger the peaks had grown. One of these foreboding crests could have swallowed up two of the hills she'd once thought were mountains at the edge of the plains near her village.

The changes must have been coming on gradually, but now the difference struck her, as though she were just waking from a sleep-deprived fog.

And maybe that was the case.

They were riding through a narrow valley that sloped

upward into a pass between the two mountains ahead, so she took the opportunity to nudge Apash forward alongside Beaver Tail's horse.

"We are nearing the land of your people?" She could sense a rider from their group pressing closer behind them and glanced over her shoulder to see Alahmoot. He'd been quiet as they rode that day, not showing any of the brashness or arrogance she'd expected from him. He kept his distance from Beaver Tail, neither speaking to the man nor being openly rude to him. That was probably the best she could hope for.

Beaver's gaze scanned the view ahead and on either side of them as he nodded. "Yes. I have ridden through these hills many times. But most of my people don't venture this deep into the mountains unless they plan to cross through to the land of your people."

War parties he meant. For the Blackfoot never came simply to trade. Did that mean Beaver Tail had been part of those raiding groups too? A disappointment slid through her. He didn't seem the sort to steal and kill without cause. Any man could change, so maybe those deeds had been in his past.

Perhaps he'd heard her thoughts, for he glanced sideways at her. "I did not come into these mountains with others, only by myself to see the land. Only one time did I pass through to the land of your people."

His words made the disappointment slide away like a cloak being shed. Once again, this brave proved a better man then she'd credited him. A snort from behind meant Alahmoot didn't agree, but neither she nor Beaver Tail turned to look at him.

Instead, she shifted her focus to important matters. "Do you think we'll soon find signs of the men we seek?"

Beaver rode quietly for a long moment. The swish of the horses' hooves in snow melded with the occasional creak of saddle leather. The constant sounds of their journey.

What thoughts ran through his mind? Did he use these quiet

moments to calculate the various trails warriors from his tribe traveled? Did he have an idea what village Telípe's kidnappers might be from?

At last, his voice broke the quiet. "I do not know which camp the warriors are from, but there are three main tracts through these mountains. Two of them come together in a place we call Two Towers. It is to that place I've been guiding us. The third trail follows a path farther north, so I don't think they would go that way."

Relief settled through her. He did have a plan. He'd been riding with the purpose.

She had counted on him getting them close to the land of the Blackfoot, then had suspected they might need to split up to search for tracks of the group they sought. But Beaver's plan sounded much better than anything she'd expected.

She nodded. "Your leading is good. How far until we reach this place, Two Towers?"

He squinted toward the sky as if he would find an answer there. And maybe he would. Maybe he could gauge from one of the distant peaks rising up into the clouds. "Two sleeps, maybe less." He shot her a look, a light twinkling in his dark eyes. "Especially if we use half of those sleeps for riding."

Again, she nodded. Speaking with Beaver Tail had eased some of the worry in her chest, but she wasn't quite ready to drop back to her place in line. Did she dare ask the other question that plagued her? What did he think was being done to her sister and the others?

In truth, she may not be able to stand it if he confirmed the awful stories she'd always heard about what Blackfoot braves did to their prisoners. He would know the truth better than anyone.

But maybe reality wasn't as bad as the tales she'd been told. Perhaps asking him would ease her fears. Did she dare?

With a breath for strength, she plunged in. "How are they

treating them do you think? My sister and the others." Should she speak of Telípe's babe? Would the Blackfoot kidnappers even know she was with child? Would that matter to them, and, if so, for the better or worse? She had to ask. "My sister carries a babe. Will her treatment be different?"

The firm lines of his jaw shifted. That couldn't be a good sign. Again, he waited long before speaking, but this time the silence didn't settle around her like a soft fur.

Tension hung thick, seeping into her with every breath, clogging her chest. The relief of learning his plan to find the group now fled as new fear wound through her.

When he spoke, his voice rumbled deep, as tight as his jaw had been. "With all peoples, there are good and bad. My tribe is no different." He glanced to her. "The same with yours, I think?"

She couldn't deny that truth.

"God made us to serve Him, but gave us our own will to choose whether we take a good path or the trail which does not please Him."

His words jumbled in her mind. God? "You mean the Great Spirit?" She'd never asked whether the Blackfoot believed in the same powers her people sought to please.

His eyes softened as he glanced her way again. "I mean the God who made us all. I once thought him only the God of the white man, but then I met Him for myself. I chose to follow His good path for me. He has a good path for all of us, no matter which tribe—white man or Indian."

The God who made us all. Beaver Tail, a Blackfoot warrior, believed in the white man's God? Could he be right that God didn't only love white men? Questions swirled in her mind, clogging her thoughts.

But Beaver Tail spoke again, and she trained her focus on his words. "You ask if I think your sister is being treated well. I do not know. I pray there are some with her who will help her."

That was an idea she'd not considered before. She'd always

thought the kidnappers would be of one mind, united in their cruelty and evil intentions. After all, would any of the braves choose to join the group unless they wanted to win captives?

A yearning rose up within her—a longing she'd felt more than once of late. If only she had a God she could pray to, One with the power to help her sister even when Meksem couldn't be there. If Beaver was right, if the God he'd chosen really did love her people as much as white men, would He accept her too?

Could she be good enough for Him?

CHAPTER 15

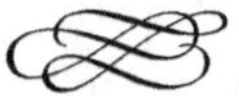

$\mathcal{A}$dam's nerves had been a jumbled ball since they left the cave the morning before. Throughout that day and this one, Tesoro plodded forward with a steady limp. Downhill seemed worse for the horse than when they had to struggle up a slope. Every time they stopped to let the animals rest, Adam packed the injuries with snow and ice.

They seemed to be stopping a little more than normal, an accommodation for which he was grateful. Of course, that didn't lessen his fear that he was slowing the group down from their goal of catching up with the kidnapping party.

When darkness had fallen, they found a quiet place to sleep a few hours, and the break seemed to help the injured gelding. Now, they were into their second day on the trail since leaving the cave.

Adam raised his gaze to the line of riders ahead of him. He'd been staring at Alahmoot's broad shoulders all morning, a sight that didn't help his mood.

Not that the man had done anything to cause Adam's jealousy. Only the fact that he was Meksem's same age, same people, and same background. Did all that make him a better fit for her? The question had Adam fighting to keep from grinding his teeth.

He had to push this jealousy aside. He didn't have the energy or mental focus right now.

But that didn't stop him from watching as the man spoke a few words to Meksem in their own language when they all dismounted for the noon meal. Even speaking to Alahmoot was more natural for Meksem. She didn't have to struggle to think of how to say the right words in his language like she did when she spoke to Adam. Why hadn't he taken the time yet to learn her tongue?

Did she prefer to speak Nimipuutímt—the language of the Nez Perce—or that of her Salish heritage? She'd grown up in the Nimiipuu camp, but her Salish father seemed important to her. Did that make his tongue more dear?

So much he didn't know, but he wanted to find out. If only they could have another day together like that long walk back after finding Tesoro. Why hadn't he spent more time asking her questions instead of telling his own story?

He'd started off talking about his and Joel's journey to open up conversation, and she truly seemed to want to hear more of his tales. The connection that grew between them as the day progressed had affected him all the way to his core.

Now, they were stopped beside a cluster of trees, and, as soon as Caleb tied his mare, he stepped into the woods. They would likely all take a turn before they finished eating and remounted.

Within minutes, Caleb emerged from the woods. "There's a little hot spring coming out of a rock on the other side of these trees. Seems just right for the horses to drink."

Adam lowered his stirrup after loosening his mount's girth, then gave the horse a pat before turning to his friend. "Sometimes they don't like the smell of the minerals, but we should try."

Caleb led the way as the group moved through the trees and up a hill to the boulder set against a cliff wall. Stone enclosed the water on three sides, almost hiding it from view. After bubbling out of the spring into a pool no bigger than the length of a man's arm, the creek had worn a deep groove into the rock bed of the mountain, flowing along the base of the cliff.

Caleb led his mare to drink first, and after she sniffed several times, she finally eased close enough to gulp in deep draughts.

"You're sure it's not too hot for her?" Adam stood with his horses at the base of the mountain to wait his turn, but even from there, he could see the steam wafting from the water's surface.

"It's just warm, not hot. Don't know why it's steaming so." Caleb patted his horse's neck as she finished drinking.

The two elder Salish men watered their mounts next, then Beaver Tail approached with his and Susanna's horses.

Meksem stood with her mare behind Adam's geldings, and he would've offered to water her horse for her, but the tight space around the pool would make it hard to manage three horses at once. Especially with Tesoro limping. Instead, when his turn came, he motioned for her to go ahead of him.

She gave a stubborn shake of her head. "You are first."

He knew better than to try to convince her, so, with a sigh, he led his geldings to the water. Tesoro drank like he hadn't seen a drop of liquid in days. "Get all you need, boy." He stroked the black spots across the horse's shoulder. He could only pray this water wasn't tainted. It had a murky smell, like rotten eggs, but the water bubbled clear.

When both his animals drank their fill, he turned and led them down the hill toward where the others had clustered to eat. He sent Meksem a smile as he passed her, but she was speaking to Alah-moot in the Salish language and didn't even seem to see Adam.

He pressed down a flare of jealousy, especially when her eyes lit as she spoke. Her expression had turned animated, and she even used her hands to accent her words.

Had he ever seen her so engaged when she spoke? He'd certainly never seen her as beautiful as now, with her eyes sparkling and a smile brightening her face. The knife of jealousy twisted harder, and he turned away before he made a fool of himself.

Maybe the man had asked about her sister. Or some other subject dear to Meksem's heart. Surely the topic she spoke of was what brought her to life, not the man who watched her with a confident half-smile on his tawny face.

After finding enough fodder for his horses to eat while they rested, he took the camas bread Susanna handed him and sank on a rock to rest himself. One would think that, after lounging in the saddle day after day, he wouldn't want to sit when given the chance to move around. But his weary muscles protested the effort that would be required to walk anywhere in this mountainous country.

He tried not to listen to the melodic murmurings of Meksem's voice as she continued speaking with Alahmoot while they watered their animals. She'd not ended the conversation when her mare finished drinking but stood nearby to hear the brave's response.

In fact, the two stood by the spring even after their horses had finished. Adam tried to press the sound of their voices from his mind, doing his best to turn his thoughts to Joel and what he might be doing. Had Elan's family been receptive of him? Had he recovered completely from his injuries?

A laugh broke through his thoughts, a sweet melodious chuckle, rich and soothing. Just as he'd imagined Meksem's laugh would sound.

His traitorous gaze turned toward the pair still standing beside the spring. Had they moved closer to each other? That knife plunged deeper, twisting in a hard swivel. He pushed to his feet. Maybe he did need to walk after all.

"I'm going to stretch my legs." He didn't meet any of the gazes that rose to him, but their heat seared him as he turned and stomped toward the trees—in the opposite direction from where Meksem stood with the man whose presence she was clearly enjoying.

His footsteps crunched loudly in the ice-crusted snow blanketing the little copse. Several limbs had fallen that would make good firewood. Too bad he hadn't grabbed the hatchet from his saddle pack. Maybe after he gave himself a few minutes to cool, he would go back for the tool and vent the rest of his frustration by cutting away branches and slicing the wood into manageable chunks.

As he stepped out of the trees on the far side and started up the hill to the trail they'd been following, he worked to take in deep breaths, letting the mountain air clear his mind as he stretched his limbs. Allowing himself to get riled over Meksem talking with another man—even one who, from an outside perspective, might seem a perfect match for her—would be foolish. If only he could clear away the image of her face so enlivened, her bright eyes, her soothing chuckle.

Thunder and lightning. This hike wasn't using up enough of his energy. The time away only gave his mind room to roam.

He spun around and marched back toward the gathering he'd just left. At least he'd tied his horses at the edge of the trees, enabling him to grab his hatchet without walking through the middle of the gathering.

Tesoro gave a low nicker of greeting when Adam approached, and he spared a moment to rub the horse's neck before taking the ax from his pack. He tried not to let his focus lift to the rest of the group sitting on various rocks while they ate. But his wayward gaze slid up once, just far enough to see that Meksem had finally rejoined the others, although the person sitting nearest her was Alahmoot.

A fresh boil of frustration surged through him, and he retreated into the woods.

He started with the first fallen limb he came to, whacking the small branches off with slicing strokes. The effort surged through his body, releasing his pent-up frustrations with every blow.

This was what he needed.

The combination of worry and frustration had probably contributed to his irrational jealousy. Every hard *thwak* of iron against wood released a little more tension. He finished with the first limb far too quickly, then moved to the next.

This log was even smaller than the first, and he made quick work of it, slicing the pieces into lengths easy to carry on the packhorses. He'd only seen one more fallen branch, so maybe after he finished cutting that one, he'd fell a small tree or two. Until Meksem called them to ride again, he'd give his body every chance to vent.

He'd just delivered the first blow to the third fallen log when a sound close behind made him spin.

Meksem.

Sunlight shone through the trees from behind her, illuminating her outline like a stained glass angel in the cathedral they'd attended back in Andalusia. She pushed her fur hood back, and the cast of light shimmered through her dark hair to form a halo. Shadows on her tawny face made her look even more exotic, clutching his breath in his chest. He had to fight to keep from pressing a hand over his heart to still the rapid beating.

The expression on her face was hard to read. Not her normal warrior's mask, this was a look more...inquisitive, maybe.

He waited for her to speak. In truth, with the churning of

thought and emotion inside him, there was no telling what words would come from his mouth. Apparently, chopping wood hadn't helped him settle his mind as much as he'd thought.

"What are you doing?" Her question was mild enough, but there was a hesitation in her words. Maybe even restraint. Because she was distancing herself from him? Or maybe she thought he'd lost his mind.

And apparently he had. His mind, his heart, and all his control. Something in him, maybe the self-destructive part, wanted to ask her what she'd been speaking of with the Salish brave. What in the great wide ocean had she found so funny she'd finally released that clear, musical laugh?

He turned back to the logs before he said something he'd regret and swung a blow that resonated through the trees. "Cutting firewood." He ground the words through a clenched jaw, then raised the hatchet for another swing.

A hand gripped his shoulder, the hold strong enough to turn him. Not the weak pull of an Indian maiden.

The clasp of a warrior.

Anger sparked in her gaze. "What is it you hide from?" She stood near enough he could feel her frustration, the emotion entangling with his own.

He reached for his own anger to ward off the other emotions sluicing through him. With a glare, he bit out his answer. "You, Meksem. And I'm not hiding." Clamping his mouth shut, he drew in a breath of icy air through his nostrils. Anything to quench the flame inside him.

She stepped nearer, the thrust of her palm on his shoulder spinning him the rest of the way to face her. Her eyes narrowed. "I don't know what you hide from. I did not think you lacked in mind or courage, but now I'm not sure."

The words struck him, and he straightened, shoring his

defenses. Preparing his own attack. But no, he couldn't attack her. Defend only.

He raised his jaw. "I don't lack either one. I'm just trying to give you space. Room to make up your own mind." There. He'd put his cards on the table. The next turn was hers, and, if she selected the obvious choice—the Salish brave sitting on the other side of these trees—he'd step away.

And pray she'd be happy.

The space between them spanned only the length of his arm. He could reach out and pull her closer, wrap one hand around her waist and weave the other through her hair, drawing her nearer. Pressing his mouth to her strong lips. Tasting her. Would she be sweet? Not like the sticky syrup of honey. More like the spicy sweetness of a rich *chorizo*.

Everything about her exuded strength…and flavor.

He jerked himself from that line of thought, then yanked his eyes from her mouth. Had she caught him looking there? What must she be thinking about his mixed messages?

He checked her eyes for any sign of her thoughts. The way her lids had narrowed, he couldn't read anything in her dark gaze. A weight pressed on his chest. Why didn't she say something? Do something? Should he speak again?

No. This was her choice. If Alahmoot would suit her better, she had to feel free to choose him. Adam couldn't influence her in any way. And besides, asking would only further reveal his weakness. If she decided against him, he needed at least a little protection for his pride.

But then, in a single action, she stepped near enough that only a handbreadth separated them. She pressed both her palms to his cheeks, pulled him down, raised her mouth to meet his.

Meksem had never kissed a man. She could barely breathe with what she was doing. This might well be the boldest action she'd ever taken, even more than stepping forward to join the warriors in the death hunt.

But she had to show Adam how wrong he was.

She'd been so caught up in telling Alahmoot the story of how Telípe and her brothers followed Meksem around when they were young, she'd not paid attention to what the rest of the group was doing. But the moment she finished the tale, she realized Adam wasn't with them. She could hear his steps in the trees though and assumed he'd only needed a private moment.

At least, that's what she told herself to push away the worry nagging at the edges of her mind.

But when he'd returned only long enough to gather his ax, then stomped off again and started the fierce chopping, as though trying to hack any tender thought for her from his heart and mind, she'd known what he was thinking.

He must have seen her talking to Alahmoot. Speaking of her sister had eased some of her pent-up worry, but Adam wouldn't have known the topic was what lightened her mood, not the person she spoke to. If he thought she could possibly choose Alahmoot, or any man, over him—then the Adam she'd come to know on this journey was more a fool then she'd meant when she goaded him with the words.

But he was no fool.

As her lips touched his, she could feel the tightening in his own. Surprise, surely.

Then, with an intake of breath, his mouth pressed against hers. The fierce energy he'd exuded as he sliced at the branches with his hatchet now channeled onto her lips. Desire swooped through her, springing her body to life in every part. She'd rebuffed every brave who'd ever tried to touch her. And now, she was so glad she'd waited for this kiss.

This man.

His hands cupped her neck, his thumbs stroking her jaw. His fingers warm and strong as they wove through the hair at the base of her head. She pressed closer to him, her body yearning for more of the life he breathed into her.

This man.

Far too soon, the intensity of his mouth softened, shifting to a gentle caress. The softer touch nearly stole the strength from her legs. She almost sagged, water in his hands. Again, she had to fight the desire to press herself closer. She'd lost every part of her control. What must he think?

But he didn't take advantage, proving once again she could trust him even when she couldn't trust herself. His mouth stilled, easing away from hers. Just enough for him to brush her nose with his, their heads resting together. His breath mingled in the air between them, and she inhaled the fragrance of the camas bread he'd eaten.

"Meksem." He spoke her name as both a groan and a prayer.

The pulsing within her flared, and she focused on the touch of his face beneath her hands. Soaking him in with every part of her senses, doing her best not to give way to her weakness.

His chest heaved as he drew in a long breath, then pulled away enough that she could see him without his face blurring before her.

Her body missed his warmth, and she lowered her hands, letting her palms slide down his chest, resting over his heart for a long moment. With her own fortifying breath, she stepped backward, pulling her hands away from him.

She raised her jaw, forcing her eyes to meet his gaze. Maybe she should be ashamed of her brash behavior, but he'd certainly returned the kiss.

He'd also been the one to end it.

She didn't let herself back down. She had to force her mind to recall the reason she'd come to him in these trees, then struggled for the right words. "I know my mind. I am not a fickle stream weaving to and fro around stones in the creek."

His gaze shifted to uncertainty. "Are you sure? You should choose what will make you happy."

How could he still question?

She raised her brows, drawing forth extra courage to tease. "Need I show you again?"

Little by little, the worry slipped from his gaze. The corners of his eyes lifted, a smile starting deep inside him, shimmering in those windows to his thoughts. "You might need to."

She willed the flush not to creep all the way up to her cheeks. No matter how she tried, she couldn't bite back a smile.

From the other side of the trees, a horse whinnied—a reminder of everyone waiting for them. For a heartbeat, she wanted to step back into Adam's arms. To hide herself away from the struggle and worry of their journey.

Maybe he saw that desire, for he stepped forward and touched her forearm, sliding his hand down to weave his fingers through hers. "We should get back."

She let herself soak in one last gaze at the strong lines of his face. She could reach up and touch his jaw if she wanted. She did want to, but she pressed that desire down and turned toward the group of people and horses on the other side of the trees.

~

*A*s the day progressed into nightfall, not even the glacial drop in temperature and the heavy sky portending snow could freeze the warmth stirring in Adam's chest.

Meksem had kissed him. She'd chosen *him*.

They hadn't reached an agreement exactly, but she seemed to have finally given herself permission to explore what could grow between them. That felt like more than a win.

It felt like a miracle.

The shy glances she sent his way throughout the afternoon stirred his blood. So unlike her warrior persona. He loved both sides of her.

Yes, *loved*.

Maybe it was too early to use that word. Maybe this sensation was only the seedling of what would grow into love, but he'd never possessed such a certainty in his chest. A knowing that stemmed from his soul.

Almighty God. Lord. He'd heard Caleb use that title for God earlier, and the word rang in his spirit. He wanted God to be his Lord in the truest sense of the word. This feeling had been growing in his heart these past days, a rightness just as strong as when he thought of Meksem in his life.

Lord, if she's the one, make my way plain. Don't let me ruin this.

"There's our snow." French stared up at the sky as they rode through the darkness.

Adam followed his gaze and eyed the peso-sized flurries floating downward. He pulled his coat tighter against the wind gusting through the mountains.

"How much farther till those two towers, BT?" Caleb called to the front of the line.

Beaver Tail turned to look back at them as his gelding plodded onward. His voice dipped much quieter than Caleb's had. "In daylight, we would see them now. We should reach them before dawn."

Adam sat a little straighter in his saddle. They all knew they might see signs of the Blackfoot party at any minute, but knowing that group would pass with almost certainty by the two towers had made that place feel special. It seemed surreal that they would reach it before daylight this night.

"Does that mean you're not gonna let us stop and sleep?" The usual rolling cadence of French's accent slurred even more in feigned exhaustion. Or maybe the real thing.

They were all weary beyond words from traveling for weeks with so little sleep. The horses had maintained surprising vigor, and the people were doing their best to keep up good spirits, even the three from Heinmot's group, although they stayed quieter than the others. The difference in language probably accounted for much of that.

Beaver turned in his saddle again and, this time, looked to Meksem. "There is a place where many camp over the next hill. There are trees to give cover from snow." His gaze flicked up to the falling flakes. "I do not think we should stay in the place most people camp, but there is another area off the trail a little farther ahead. It would not be safe to have a fire because we might be seen, but we can rest there."

Meksem nodded. "A good plan."

As the night sounds drifted around them, Adam strained to pick out the source of each. The hoot of an owl. In the distance, either the howl of a wolf or the screech of a mountain lion. The animal was too far away to distinguish for certain.

And always the steady swish of horse hooves against snow and the faint squeak of saddle leather. Most of their equipment was so worn and saturated with grease, it didn't make a sound. But every few minutes, a bit of leather would squeeze against another to produce a creak.

After an hour, or maybe two, they'd almost reached the top of the hill Beaver had mentioned. The man threw up his hand to signal a halt as he reined his horse in.

Adam sat deep in his saddle to stop his own horses as the others did the same. Beaver stared hard at the ground, and Adam fought the urge to nudge his mount forward to see what the man had noticed. There wasn't room enough on the trail for him to lead both his horses around the line of riders.

"Horse tracks." Beaver spoke the word just above a whisper as he studied first the ground beside him, then the path ahead.

Meksem had ridden up beside him, and the two communicated in low whispers as Beaver motioned ahead of them. With a nod, she answered, then pushed her horse forward into a quick jog.

Adam's heart surged in his chest. Surely she wasn't going ahead to seek out danger. He couldn't help himself as he handed Tesoro's tether strap to Caleb. "Hold him for a minute." Caleb took the lead without questioning, and Adam nudged his mount forward until he reached Beaver Tail's side.

His friend didn't seem surprised to see him and even saved Adam the trouble of asking. "She goes to scout the camping place."

Adam forced back the worry threatening to overwhelm his good sense and scanned the ground to find the tracks Beaver had seen.

They were only faint indentations in the snow but just about the right size and shape to be horse hooves. The snow falling these past hours had filled in the prints some, but not completely.

Finally he allowed himself a question but did his best to strip his tone of any anger. "Would it not have been safer for you to ride ahead, since you know this land?"

"It is her sister we seek. She must make her own way. I follow her lead."

Adam clamped his mouth shut. Beaver Tail was right, of course. But that didn't stop his overwhelming urge to protect Meksem.

"She is capable." Beaver Tail's soft murmur wove through him, settling amid the worry churning in his mind.

He inhaled a deep breath to soak in the truth of the words.

"And God is with her. He goes before us when we ask Him to."

That final thought eased the last of Adam's fears, replacing them with the certainty that could only come from God. He blew out a breath. "You're right."

Go before her, Lord. Guide her steps, give her wisdom.

A new thought wove through his mind, one separate from their current situation. Or, maybe not.

Which God did Meksem follow?

She'd asked him that question, but he'd been so in awe of the way God had saved Tesoro that day, he'd not thought to ask her the same. How could he have neglected a question so important? An urgency rose inside him to ride forward and ask her now. To tell her of the God Who could go before them and fight their battles. To make her see that He was greater than any deity she'd been taught to worship.

He would have to wait.

Another hour seemed to pass as Beaver Tail kept them moving forward at a steady walk. When they crested the rise, he slowed them just long enough to scan the trees covering the downward slope for any sign of movement. His voice dropped to a half whisper. "We'll meet her just inside those woods."

As Adam nodded, he strained to see or hear any sign of her

coming. She and her mare both moved quietly, as though the horse were an extension of the woman.

When they entered the shelter of the trees, the snow tapered to a light dusting, leaving thicker darkness than before.

His horse pricked its ears, and Adam tensed. Even listening so hard, he didn't hear Meksem coming before she and her horse appeared through the night shadows.

Some of the tension slipped from his shoulders, and he scanned her face for a sign of what she'd seen. No excitement marked her features.

Even though she was a master at disguising her thoughts, she wouldn't have reason to cover the joy of finding her sister, would she?

As Meksem reined her horse in front of them, she shook her head. "There is no one at the camping place. The tracks ride past without stopping."

She turned her mare and started back the way she'd just come, and he and Beaver fell in behind her, the others tracking behind them.

He couldn't help the sense of foreboding that wove through him. Was someone watching them from just out of sight? Maybe he was simply paranoid, but he moved his gelding closer to Beaver Tail and spoke in a low murmur. "Could someone be watching us? Should we split up so we're not as easy to spot?"

One wrong move could warn the Blackfoot party of their presence and make them lose any upper hand that surprise might offer.

Or the Blackfoot could attack them instead. For that matter, the kidnappers could simply steal away in the darkness with their captives.

Being attacked by the Blackfoot might be the best of those options. At least then they could meet the men head on.

Beaver didn't look at him as he answered in the same low tone. "Maybe. There are so many of us, it's hard to hide us all. I think it's better to stay together so we don't risk shooting one of our own group."

A valid point. In the dark woods, it would be hard to know whether a rustle was caused by one of their own party or the enemy.

They rode on together, keeping to the trail with weapons at the ready. Beaver Tail, Susanna, French, Caleb, and Adam all carried guns. Meksem and the three Salish braves held their bows in hand.

He might have wondered why Meksem didn't have an arrow at the ready, but he'd seen her draw from the quiver strapped to her back, notch the end in the bowstring, and send it sailing—all in the blink of an eye. Maybe she'd practiced the action so much, she was faster with the arrows stored in the quiver.

She had shifted into her warrior persona, her face a hard mask, eyes seeing everywhere at once.

Her strength and bravery resonated through every movement, but he didn't let himself look at her very often.

He had to keep his focus on their surroundings. The danger was too great to let this lady warrior distract him.

CHAPTER 17

*A*dam easily spotted the camping area when they finally reached the place. A small, level area clear of trees, with snow mounded higher near the middle, probably covering coals from many previous fires. But Meksem had been right that the faint dips in the snow marking tracks didn't stop here.

Their group didn't stop either, as Meksem kept her mare moving down the trail.

Beaver Tail nudged his horse alongside Meksem, then pointed toward the trees on his left. He turned his mount off the path in that direction, Meksem slipping her horse in behind his. They wound through the woods for several minutes, not following any path that Adam could see. Then the trees opened up into a small clearing.

Beaver halted his horse to one side so the others could gather. "This is a good place to sleep. A fire would be too risky, though."

"At least the snow is slowing." Caleb slid down from his saddle with a weary sigh. "Think we should set a watch?"

Part of Adam sagged at the suggestion. The same idea had slipped through his mind, and having someone stand guard would be a wise move. But they were all working under such a minimal amount of sleep already. They usually slept about four hours each night, so maybe they could each take an hour's watch?

When he voiced the thought, the others agreed quickly. Within minutes, they'd settled the animals and laid out a few furs to sleep on. Adam took the food Susanna offered and tried not to tear into it as his hungry belly chose that moment to growl. When this was all over, he'd sleep for a week and fill his stomach with as much warm grub as it wanted. Hopefully, he'd be tucked inside a lodge with a cozy fire burning.

Maybe back in Meksem's village? What else would be different by then? He couldn't let himself follow that train of thought. His weary mind might form all manner of images that would set his heart up for disappointment.

One step at a time. Telípe first, then he and Meksem would have more time to explore what was growing between them.

Alahmoot took the first watch, and, as they all bedded down, Meksem offered Adam one side of the buffalo robe they'd shared before. His heart leapt at the thought, but something in his spirit raised a warning. He had to be careful to keep things above reproach between him and Meksem.

Sure, they'd shared the buffalo robe cover when sleeping upright by the fire. But there hadn't been this humming aware-ness between them, at least not as much as now stirred every time their gazes met, even across a distance. They had room to stretch out in this little clearing, so everyone was lying down to sleep. Would it be indecent to share a blanket with Meksem while lying down?

He met her gaze with a slight shake of his head. "I think I'd better use my own covering tonight." He watched for signs she understood his meaning. Her eyes were hard to read, but her gaze didn't show hurt.

Then some of the warrior's mask slipped from her eyes, and

he could see the longing there. He stepped near, everything in him wanting to touch his hand to her cheek. To lower his mouth and taste the wonder of her lips again.

But the others were so near. Was this what Beaver Tail had to contend with every day? The man must have the self-control of a martyr.

Then an idea slipped in. He took the fur from her hands and laid the bundle on the bedding she'd already stretched across the ground. "Come with me to make sure Tesoro's secure for the night."

The corners of her mouth tipped, and she gave a slight nod. They'd not done anything in front of the others to give hint of their growing feelings, but he was pretty sure most of the group had caught on. These friends were savvy, no doubt.

As they slipped into the trees, he reached out a gloved hand, and Meksem fit her fur-clad fingers around his. Ducking under branches, they wove around the other animals until they reached Tesoro. Plenty of barriers stood between them and the rest of the group, and if they kept their voices low they shouldn't be heard, much less seen.

Maybe he should have started by checking the horse as he said he would, but he couldn't stand another minute with this woman so near. He spun to her and stepped close, raising his hands to cup her face as he'd been craving. She already had her own palms pressed to his shoulders, lifting her face to his.

Her eyes found his in the sliver of moonlight, and he soaked in her beautiful gaze. For a long moment, he let his eyes drink, then finally lowered his lids and took her mouth with his.

Heaven. Her lips had been soft and pliant this morning, but now she kissed with a passion that flamed through him. As though she'd been longing for this as much as he had.

He wove his fingers deep through her hair, and with his other hand wrapped her waist and pulled her close. She pressed against him, fueling his fire and stealing his breath as he deepened the kiss still more. He'd never been so consumed, so completely unaware of anything around them. Her touch lit him in a thousand different places.

If he didn't stop now, he would lose control completely. So much of him wanted to lose control.

But he couldn't. *God, help me. I can't.*

He summoned every bit of his strength and tore his mouth from hers, heaving in deep breaths of frosty air to clear his head.

He couldn't quite bring himself to let her go, but he did ease back a little. Enough to put a sliver of space between them.

She was breathing hard too, and her eyes held that glazed look. Her lips, though…her lips. He couldn't look at them again. He'd not be able to resist their swollen luxury.

He pulled his gaze back up to her eyes. "Meksem." The out-of-control feeling was fading, and, as the sensation seeped away, so did the strength from his limbs. He dropped his forehead to rest on hers and moved both of his hands to her upper back, rubbing circles with his thumbs. She might not feel the pressure through her thick coat, but he suspected she would. He could feel every breath she took, every shift, every thought.

For a long moment, they stood like that, breathing each other in. Could she possibly feel half as much for him as he did for her? He lifted his head enough to focus on her face.

He struggled for the right words, ones that would make her understand his meaning clearly. "I never thought I could feel this way about a woman. You're quickly becoming one of the most important things in my life."

She stared at him a long moment, and he willed her to understand the meaning of his heart. Her thoughts were hard to read in her gaze, though. Had she slipped the warrior mask back in place? No, this wasn't that fierce façade. This was…uncertainty?

Sure. He was moving way too fast. He was the kind of man

to make up his mind and take action, but that didn't mean she was ready for that next step. Hadn't he already told himself he would wait until after they finished this business with Telípe?

But here he was, stepping ahead of himself, just like he'd done when he'd ridden Tesoro. He shifted his hands to take a gentle hold on her upper arms. "I don't want to rush you, Meksem. There's much happening right now. We can talk more later."

She dropped her gaze then, lowered her chin and turned to stare sideways at Tesoro. Maybe not at Tesoro exactly. Her mind seemed to have wandered far away.

He had no idea what she might be thinking, and the not knowing pressed an ache hard in his chest. He resisted the urge to prod her, holding himself still. But he didn't drop his hands from her arms.

This would be a good time to take a different kind of action. *Lord, show me what she needs. Don't let me run ahead of Your plan here. Guide her. Guide us both.*

Meksem still stared in the direction of Tesoro, and finally she spoke, her tone so soft he had to strain to make out her words. "The only other man I've loved left me."

The only other man she'd *loved*? Did that mean she loved him? Yet there was another before him?

She turned to face him then, and lines of sadness fanned around her eyes. "He died when I was five. My father looked at me the way you do, seeing the real me." Her throat worked.

Maybe it was as dry as his own had become. He wanted to cradle her close, to soothe away the overwhelming sadness she must feel, the same as what pressed on his own heart.

But she was speaking again. "It hurt so much to lose him. I told myself I would never feel that pain again." Her voice shook on those last few words. Her pain twisted through him, and he had to fight down the burn in his eyes.

She paused long enough to take a full breath and release the spent air. Her eyes searched his as though trying to discover whether he would put her through that same pain she'd suffered at her father's passing.

Then a half-cry, half-laugh slipped from her throat. "I don't even have the tomahawk anymore, the last gift he gave me. I don't know if I can handle—" She cut off her words, but he knew what she would've said.

He slipped one of his hands up to cup her cheek, wishing his glove didn't separate him from the softness there. He met her gaze and willed her to believe the words he would speak. "I don't want you to lose me, Meksem. I promise that the only way you will is if God takes me Himself."

Her eyes glimmered, filling with liquid. "But that's how I lost my father."

Her agony speared through him. He pulled her close, wrapping her tight in his arms. With a deep breath, he inhaled the rich scent of her hair. "I don't have control over that. I can only trust God to keep us both in His hand. But I know He does. He'll keep his protection around us." Certainty slipped through him, an absolute knowing that his words were true. They *were* in God's hand.

Meksem pulled back, but only far enough to see his face. "Beaver Tail said he chose to follow your God. To take the good path God made for him. Do you believe your God has that path for everyone? Even my people?"

Hope flickered inside him. This was the moment he'd been hoping for. "I do. There's no doubt in my mind He wants you for His daughter. He has a path for you." He couldn't help adding, "And I pray that path is alongside mine."

She gave a slow, single nod. But her eyes still clouded with emotion. She might need time to make her decision. At least she was asking the right questions.

For now, they needed to get back to the others. At this rate, the time for his watch might come before he bedded down. But there was one lingering question pressing against his mind.

He dipped his head. "What did you mean about a tomahawk?" Her eyes had filled with so much pain when she'd mentioned it. He'd never heard her speak of anything like that before.

A guarded look slipped through her eyes. "It was...a gift my father gave me at the end."

A sick feeling spread through his gut. He was almost afraid to voice his next question. "And you don't have it anymore?"

She moved her head in a slight shake, and her lips pressed together. Her gaze hovered somewhere around his nose. A sure sign she didn't want to tell him something.

That sour sensation in his belly spread up into his chest. He wanted to make her look in his eyes but wasn't sure he could bring himself to see her pain when she answered his next question. "You traded it for Tesoro, didn't you?

She turned away, looking beyond the horse again. Combined with her silence, the action told him all he needed to know. Anger sluiced through him. Her father's last gift to her, something she must have treasured with immeasurable value. What could have caused her to exchange it for a gift for him? Even a horse this magnificent.

She'd traded her father's legacy.

His breaths came fast. The pain spreading through his extremities had no choice but to come out. But the emotion had twisted into anger. She shouldn't have given up something so precious for him, even for this incredible horse. Yet, he couldn't show frustration to Meksem. He couldn't respond with fury to a sacrifice so great. He struggled for control over his voice.

"Meksem. I don't..." He took in a slow breath. The act was done, chastising her wouldn't change anything. When they returned to the land of her people, maybe he could get the tomahawk back. He blew the breath out in a long stream. "Thank you." That was the tone he needed.

She glanced back at him, her expression hesitant. He softened his gaze and his voice even more. "Your sacrifice means more to me than I can say."

With a nod, she looked away again. He turned with her, releasing her with one hand and slipping his other around her waist to pull her close to his side.

She didn't stiffen but sank against him as if she'd been fashioned to fit there. Still, the silence lingered over them. He couldn't let Meksem lose such a special gift from her father. Maybe it would take time for him to fix it, but at least he knew the truth now.

He pressed a kiss to her forehead and gave her a gentle squeeze. "We should get back."

As one, they headed toward the soft sounds of steady breathing. The night would be even shorter now, and he needed to focus all his attention on preparing for the challenge ahead.

CHAPTER 18

*A*dam had volunteered for the third watch. Not a preferred turn, for it meant his sleep would be broken into parts. But he wouldn't allow himself an easier shift than any of the others.

When French woke him, he could hardly believe he'd gone to sleep, cold as he was. Snow fell in a steady sheet, but at least the wind didn't blow through the trees.

He pushed to his feet, taking the elk hide with him to wrap around his shoulders. Even sleeping in his coat and hood and gloves and moccasins, he couldn't feel his fingers or toes. "You see or hear anything?"

French stood like a weary soldier, so tired Adam might need to turn and point him toward his bed pallet. The man shook his head. "Only a little rustling that turned out to be our horses. Not even any night birds." He shuffled toward his blankets. "Enjoy your turn."

Adam watched the man collapse onto his bedding. This journey had stretched them all, and he could only pray they hadn't reached their breaking point. Things were bound to get worse before they finished the mission.

With his rifle in hand, he scanned each person in the clearing, doing a mental headcount. All there.

Then he focused his attention on the darkness weaving through the trees around them. Nothing looked irregular. No sounds pricked his worry. He should check the horses too. He'd been sidetracked by Meksem before and didn't actually confirm Tesoro's tie was secure. But the animal had mellowed so much with his injury and the long days on the trail, he wasn't likely to wander away. Especially when there wasn't the howling of the storm whipping around them like that other time. This snowfall, although thick, was as gentle as a white blanket settling over the ground.

The horses slept as he approached, all tied to separate trees. Meksem's mare snuffled when he stroked her neck, and so did one of the other spotted horses, either Yaka's or Ukugnut's. It was hard to tell them apart in the thick darkness without saddles. The rest of the animals were so weary they barely flicked an ear when he stopped to greet them.

He rounded the big mare Caleb rode and finally came in view of his own horses through the thick snowfall. He squinted past the spots dancing across his gaze. Only his riding gelding stood tied to the tree. The last vestige of sleep sprang off Adam as his heart pounded hard in his ears.

Where was Tesoro? Maybe the horse had shifted so he stood deeper in the shadows.

He strode forward, barely checking his desire to yell out for the horse. There was always the possibility the enemy lurked nearby. Maybe Tesoro had been stolen. Adam had to keep his wits about him and stay quiet.

He crept to the tree where he'd tied the horse. The trunk stood barren, but the ground had been stomped into a mess of hoof prints. He scanned the woods all around, peering through the falling flakes. "Tesoro?" He kept his voice low.

Of course, the animal didn't answer. And no other sounds

met his straining ears. He dropped his gaze to the ground. There were so many tracks, both from the horse and human prints from him and the others checking the horses. But only a single set of horse tracks walked away, although the new snow was quickly filling them.

Adam followed the trail the horse had made, bending low to see the prints in the darkness. But even with the branches he had to continually duck, he was able to move quickly.

He would only go a short distance to see if Tesoro had stayed close by. He couldn't tell how long ago the horse had left. French said he'd checked the animals, but had he counted them all to make sure none were missing? Had that been an hour ago? The tracks could be that old, depending on how long the snow had been falling so thickly.

Whatever had possessed the horse to leave this time? Was he looking for fodder? Adam still hadn't completely ruled out the possibility someone had stolen him. Even if the person hadn't come planning malice toward their group, Tesoro's markings made him desirable. A man would have to be blind not to appreciate the horse, and if thieving was already a way of life...

But he didn't see human tracks next to the dips in the snow marking Tesoro's prints. Maybe the man had climbed atop the gelding back at the tree? Surely Tesoro wouldn't allow that. Except his spunk had diminished a great deal these past few days. Maybe a capable horseman could've managed riding him.

And if the thief rode Tesoro, there would be no human prints to know for sure.

Fear gripped tighter in his chest as his thoughts swirled almost out of control. He had to get a better handle on himself. He'd trekked at least ten minutes from their camp, and any hope of quickly finding the gelding had dwindled away. He didn't dare go farther without letting the others know what happened and where he was going. And he'd make better time in the saddle than on foot.

Turning back from his pursuit felt like giving up, but he upped his pace into a run and covered the ground in less than half the time.

Part of him wanted to wake Meksem and set off on the same adventure they had before, but she needed sleep. In truth, he hated to wake anyone, but Beaver Tail had volunteered for the final watch, so he would be the best one to alert.

The man awoke as Adam stepped near him, his warrior instincts springing to life. Adam crouched and explained the situation quickly. "I hope to be back within the hour. He can't have gone far."

"Any sign he was taken?" Beaver Tail kept his voice as quiet as Adam had. Beside him, Susanna didn't stir.

"Not that I can see. No human prints. He might have just gotten hungry. Maybe chewed the knot loose from around the tree." Like the horse French had told them about. The thought eased a little bit of worry from his chest.

But not much. If something happened to Tesoro... Now that he knew Meksem had traded her most prized possession, the last gift from the father she adored, he couldn't let anything happen to the horse.

He pushed to standing and turned away. Within minutes, he had his gelding saddled and his furs packed, along with the bit of food Beaver Tail brought him. If anything delayed him, he was fully supplied with everything he'd need for a day or so.

Surely that wouldn't happen. But what if Tesoro was injured again? Much worse this time?

He slammed the door on those thoughts and sent a final nod to Beaver Tail. "I'll be back soon."

Snow still fell in a thick coat as he quickly covered the ground he'd already traveled twice. Tesoro's tracks were almost impossible to recognize now, a fact that tightened the worry in his chest even more.

When he reached the end of his own prints, he had to slow

his mount and study the ground to find the spotted gelding's trail. The animal seemed to be heading in the general direction they'd been traveling before they camped. Maybe a little more north, which meant he would probably cross the trail they'd been on.

After a quarter hour or so, he could no longer find Tesoro's tracks at all. He reined in his mount and tried to press down the panic welling in his chest as he stared into the woods around him. He couldn't see much other than tall, lanky trees with scrawny limbs. Was that a mountain rising in the distance? Or maybe one of the boulders marking the twin towers Beaver had spoken of?

It was impossible to tell for sure, especially in the dark with snow still falling. But the landmark—whether it actually was one of the towers or just another cluster of trees—lay somewhat in the direction Tesoro had been traveling. Adam nudged his mount forward, letting the horse travel with the flow of the land. Hopefully this was what Tesoro would have done as well.

Their path wound a little as he rode. The pillar he'd thought he saw before reappeared several times, a little clearer at each viewing. He still couldn't think of a good reason why the horse would have wandered so far unless hunger drove him.

Or unless a stranger guided him from atop the animal's back.

Adam kept his mount at a steady walk, the fastest pace he dared so he could still keep a close eye on their surroundings. He also had to make sure he didn't guide the horse over a cluster of hidden rocks or some other danger.

They seemed to be winding through a valley, or maybe a dry streambed. He could only pray this wasn't a frozen river they might fall through, but the flow of the ground made that look unlikely. The land he traveled sloped upward a little, and every so often he caught sight of the distant boulder rising up. There must be another near it, since the place was called Two Towers, but he'd not seen the second yet.

How long had he been riding now? At least an hour. The ground sloped upward more now than before, and the trees had thinned, allowing an icy wind to buffet him. Its frigid fingers crept in around his neck, numbing his face, and even pressing through his buckskin leggings. Maybe he should get out some furs to wrap around himself. But in truth, he was too cold to move, any shift allowed the glacial winds better access to cracks in his covering.

So he hunkered low in his saddle, keeping his eyes and ears tuned to movement or sounds around him. Not an easy feat with his hood pulled as far over his head as he could manage. He had to turn in the saddle often to look around him.

His horse gave notice of the sound first, pricking its ears toward something ahead. Adam focused his attention that direction and tightened his reins to slow the gelding. He could see nothing except the same upward slope covered in trees they'd been following for a while now.

The distant rocky tower was closer than before and looked to be near the top of the hill they were plodding up. Did his mount hear someone near the tower? Or maybe Tesoro had found a tree covered in tasty bark at the top of the incline.

The worry twisting in Adam's belly pulled tighter as he debated whether he should keep going on horseback or leave the gelding here and continue on foot. Alone, he could move out of the dip that served as something of a trail and into the thicker woods, then shift from tree to tree. Anyone watching for him might see him, but maybe his approach wouldn't catch the notice of the group not looking for him.

Better to take every precaution he could, since he had no idea what he was up against. Moving the gelding up the right embankment, he found a place where the horse should be comfortable enough and somewhat hidden by the scraggly branches of a thick cedar nearby. The weary gelding dropped his head as Adam tied the reins. He gave the animal a pat. "I'll be back soon, boy."

With his rifle in one hand and his shot bag and rope looped around his shoulder, he started up the hill again. Moving parallel to the path he'd been taking through the dry creek bed, he shifted from one trunk to the next. The trees stood close enough to give decent shelter, but he was traveling slower than he'd been when riding a straight path on horseback.

Even though his body had sprung to alert, propelling him forward, he was breathing hard as he neared the top of the slope. Maybe it was his imagination, but the ground definitely seemed to grow steeper as he went.

The rock tower loomed larger now, and the second one appeared a little behind the first. As he was preparing to crest the top of the hill that would make him visible to anyone up there, he paused behind a wide trunk to listen.

Was that the murmur of voices? He held his breath, straining with everything in him to hear. Yes. Or maybe…

Now the sound had stopped. Maybe the noise had been his imagination, but he had to proceed as though the Blackfoot war party was camped here. Should he ride back and get the others? Better to scout the area first, then decide what should be done next.

He moved slower now, sliding from one tree to the next, then pausing to find his next mark. He stayed low too. The snow had mostly stopped falling, which took away some of his cover. He'd have to rely on his own stealth and the dark night. At least he'd be able to see better without the falling flakes.

When he reached the point where he'd thought he would be at the top of the hill, the ground continued a lesser slope upward. But he could almost see the base of the first tower.

He hadn't yet spotted any sign of people. It might be too

much to hope that they'd have a campfire. No scent of smoke hovered in the air.

The night was so frigid, he could only pray the captives had enough furs to keep them warm. The trees grew less dense as he neared the towers, and the woods ended completely about ten strides away from the first rock face. He had to be even more careful as he proceeded.

Little by little, he made his way forward. A few more sounds carried through the air—the low rumble of male voices, but only in quick bursts. A sentence or two at a time.

His heart thumped faster each time the voices came. Had he found the Blackfoot war party? Maybe Tesoro had led him right to their target.

But then his throat tightened as reality sank in. Tesoro must be with these men. Not only would they have to free the three women and one child, they'd have to capture his horse back too.

CHAPTER 19

*A*dam paused behind a tree and peered around the trunk to scan the landscape ahead. Where were the horses?

The people and their mounts must be hidden in the woods. Before starting forward again, he took one more look around in every direction, tapping into all of his senses to see if his instincts picked up anything strange. Far to the east, the black sky faded to a dim gray, the sign that morning would come within an hour or so.

Had the others already started after him? His heart surged at the thought. He needed to warn them. If they followed his tracks up this hill, they might ride directly into the middle of the Blackfoot camp.

But, no. Meksem and Beaver Tail wouldn't allow the group to charge up the hill without caution. They would find his riding horse tied and know to be careful. He'd have to listen for them though.

He crept forward, straining to catch any sign of people.

There. That shifting through the trees must be someone. Adam froze behind a wide pine and eased his head around to see.

Definite movement there, maybe several people. That had to be their camp. Would they have a lookout posted? Probably not this far into their own territory.

Unless they really had taken Tesoro. Then, they'd be on their guard. But would they have stayed around if they'd stolen the horse? It seemed like they would be riding as far and fast as they could. Maybe these warriors were so cocksure that they didn't fear retaliation.

In that case, he should expect them to at least have a guard posted.

He had to scout the camp to make sure this was the group they'd been looking for. And maybe he could get a glimpse of the captives to make sure they weren't hurt. Perhaps he could gather details that would help his fellow rescuers put together a plan for rescue.

Adam checked his gun to make sure the weapon was ready, then gripped it tightly with both hands, his palms in position on the stock and barrel so he could shoot at a second's notice.

Then, he crept forward again. Shifting from tree to tree, pausing to find his next mark and to check for signs that he'd been noticed, then scooting forward again.

He could hear the voices louder than before, but he didn't know the language. Too bad Beaver Tail wasn't with him. Only the deep timbre of men sounded. No women or children.

A horse whinnied ahead of him, and Adam craned around a tree to find the source. The nicker had been higher pitched than Tesoro's. Once he was certain who the group was, he'd check for guards and creep around to look in on the horses.

After making his way to three more trees, he was near enough to discern some of the figures. Also near enough for them to see him if he didn't duck low.

From behind the trunk of a leafless Aspen, he eased down to his knees in the snow. Then he peered around the tree and focused on the figures in the little group. Wrapped in furs as they were, he had to study each person to determine if he gazed at warrior or squaw.

All five of the figures he saw were men. And they all lounged in a little group, several of them eating. Were they waiting for someone? Or just readying themselves for the day's journey?

He'd have to move to a different tree for a view of the areas concealed from him now. If this was the band they sought, there should be at least two more men, plus the captives.

Bending low, he worked his way on all fours to a tree on his right. From that perspective, he couldn't see any new people, but a stack of furs lay on one side of the camp. Maybe the hides covered someone still asleep.

He dropped low again and crawled toward another tree, keeping about the same distance from the camp but moving in the direction of the place where the furs sat.

Before he reached his next tree, one of the men spoke. Adam froze, not daring to breathe as he strained to pick out words. The sounds started as guttural noises that rose into a series of high–low pitches. Beaver Tail's voice sometimes carried that same cadence, even when he spoke English.

Adam hadn't yet made it to the next tree, and he'd never felt so exposed, stretched out with only a bit of low brush to separate him from the camp. But he waited for what would happen next. One of the others would probably respond. Or maybe the man who spoke was telling the others he'd seen a movement in the trees.

Adam's arms quivered from holding himself up on hands and toes, his belly only a handbreadth above the ground. Slowly, he lowered himself to the snow. Better that movement than to collapse onto the crunchy layer of ice.

He eased his head to the side so he could see what was happening in the camp. Another man spoke, turning his focus to the trees opposite Adam. Maybe the direction of the horses.

A rustle sounded just before movement flashed. Figures stepped through the tree shadows to join the group of men.

A woman, clad in buckskins and without the benefit of furs for warmth. Her hands were hidden behind her back, tied most likely. Her shoulders slumped, and she stumbled forward. It was then he saw the figure behind her. Another woman, who must have stumbled first, bumping into the one in front. Then two more figures stepped from the shadows, the first much smaller than the other three. These had to be the captives.

The fifth and final figure stepping from the dark tree cover *did* wear a fur coat. His height and bearing proclaimed him a brave—a large man who towered over the women and child shuffling ahead of him.

Adam shifted his focus back to the four smaller figures who'd sunk to the ground, huddled together, likely for both warmth and safety. The smallest had to be Yaka's son, a child around the age of five.

He scanned the faces of the three women, trying to pick out which one was Telípe and which was the boy's mother.

He couldn't tell for sure. The mother must be one of the two on either side of the lad. Probably not the woman sitting in front, who didn't look much more than a girl herself. Maybe she was Ukugnut's daughter?

He scanned the squaws on either side of the boy one more time. Surely Meksem's sister would bear some resemblance to her, although they only shared the same mother. Which of Meksem's features had she inherited from her mother, and which from the man whose loss had impacted her life so strongly?

Adam couldn't see either of the women from the front. He'd have to find out their identities later. For now, he had to plan the best way to free them. He probably couldn't do it alone, but he could gather all the information possible about their situation and captors before he went back for the others.

The five men who'd been sitting now moved into action and looked to be packing things to break camp. The brave who'd brought the captives from the trees tossed a small bundle to the younger woman with a few grunted words.

She didn't meet his gaze but began dividing the bundle into portions that she handed to the others. He couldn't tell for sure what it was—some kind of food, for they began eating. There sure wasn't much of the stuff.

The men were definitely packing, which meant they'd be leaving soon. Urgency pressed in Adam's chest. He still didn't know where the seventh man was nor whether they had possession of Tesoro. But he had to get to the rest of his group so they wouldn't lose their chance to take back these captives.

Holding his breath, he lifted himself just above the snow and eased backward to the tree that had sheltered him last. No one saw him, thank the Lord. He turned and worked his way on all fours away from the activity in the camp.

Every movement he made thundered loud in his ears. Was he moving too fast? All someone had to do was train their focus his direction and surely they would see him darting from tree to tree. He tried to force himself to move slowly, but every moment mattered. They couldn't lose this group.

And they wouldn't.

He forced himself to think rationally. The snow had all but stopped, and, especially with daylight, tracks would be easy to follow. Keeping himself from being noticed was of the utmost importance right now.

When he could no longer see or hear the Blackfoot men, he turned his focus from stealth to speed, charging forward in a sprint. Keeping to the thicker tree cover, he did his best to make his footfalls light. Within minutes, he'd reached his horse.

The animal stood quietly with its head ducked low, not even flicking an ear when Adam approached. With the gelding so tired and energy flooding his own veins, perhaps he'd do better on foot.

He pushed the thought away. He had to be ready for anything, and the horse could be spurred into a run if necessary.

"Sorry, old boy." He patted the animal as he untied the reins, then mounted in a smooth motion.

The horse required encouragement to push into a trot, but they were moving downhill, so the going wasn't hard. Even as they retraced their earlier tracks, Adam scanned the woods ahead to see if he could spot a shorter route. But he didn't dare leave the trail he'd taken to get here. The others would probably be following his prints, and he couldn't risk missing them.

~

*A*nger roiled in Meksem's chest, but she kept her jaw locked to hold the emotion in. What had Adam been thinking to ride out on his own?

Why had she ever given him that horse? The animal had caused them nothing but trouble.

Even as the thought rose up, she pressed it down. She didn't regret giving Adam the spotted gelding. Not when the animal clearly brought him so much joy.

And heartache. Was the former enough to justify all the pain Adam had experienced with the animal? All the frustration the horse had brought each time he escaped or sent Adam sailing through the air, causing pain and injuries that lasted for days.

Would Adam rather be without the beautiful animal he'd named Treasure, just so he could avoid the trials? She knew beyond a doubt he wouldn't. He loved that horse.

In truth, he might even be willing to give his life for the horse. He certainly wouldn't begrudge a little pain and frustration—or rather, a *lot* of pain and frustration.

Was all love worth the agony that came along with the good parts?

Even now, the feelings stirring inside her for Adam pressed an ache in her chest. Could she bring herself to risk loving him, knowing how easy it would be to lose him?

She would have to come to terms with the truth that she likely *would* lose him at some point. She couldn't let herself get angry every time he did something that put him in danger, whether she deemed that act too bold or foolish for her liking.

Adam loved adventure even more than she did. She would have to make peace with that part of him if they were to have any future together.

I can only trust God to keep us both in His hand. He'll keep his protection around us. Adam's words drifted through her mind.

That might be the only way she could find that peace. By putting him in the hands of his God. By trusting.

Did that mean she also had to trust her own life into God's hands? Maybe she didn't have to, but she wanted to.

She raised her gaze to the gray sky above, dawn's light filtering through the clouds. *I don't know what I must do to choose Your path. But I want to.*

A peace settled over her with the silent words. She'd made the choice. She'd have to ask Beaver Tail what else she should do to be accepted by his God.

To make Him her God.

But the rightness that came with the decision filled her chest. A new strength seeped through her veins, and she inhaled new breath as she turned her focus forward.

A glance at the ground showed they were still following Adam's tracks. The night snow must have covered Tesoro's, but Adam's trail moved forward with purpose, so he must have had the gelding's prints to lead him.

Apash's ears pricked, and all of Meksem's senses sprang to

life. She peered through the gray light at the trees ahead, preparing her hand to reach for an arrow if necessary.

Then her gaze caught on a figure sitting atop a horse in the shadows of the distant trees. Adam.

She eased out a breath, all her anger fleeing with the spent air. Only relief weighed her as she nudged her mare faster.

He'd stopped his horse but now pushed the gelding forward. Urgency marked his actions, yet the terrain between them forced them all to keep to a walk. Murmurs behind her told her the others had caught sight of him as well.

"I found them." Adam spoke almost before he was near enough for her to hear.

Her mind took a heartbeat to process that he spoke of more than just the horse he'd been seeking.

Then hope sprung inside her. "You found my sister?"

He nodded as he reined in before them. Beaver Tail moved alongside her, and she could feel the others crowding close behind. They all waited for Adam to share details.

He seemed to need a moment to catch his breath, and she had to use all her focus to wait quietly. "In the trees near the tallest rock tower. They were breaking camp. I saw six braves and the three women and boy."

"My daughter? She is well?" Ukugnut pushed forward, moving his horse to Meksem's other side. His voice trembled with strain as he spoke the choppy words in Adam's tongue.

Adam shifted his focus to the man. "None of them looked injured. One of the braves brought them back to camp while I watched, then gave them food to eat."

A tremor of relief slipped through Meksem. Telípe was well. Or at least, not so hurt that her injury was obvious. And they were feeding the captives, that was good.

But the deep grooves marking Adam's brow told her she still had much to worry about.

CHAPTER 20

Meksem watched as Adam turned his horse back in the direction he'd come from. "They're probably already on the trail. We need to hurry."

She nudged her mare into step behind his gelding, and the group rode single file as they retraced his tracks. She kept all of her senses alert, especially when they moved uphill and the rock towers came into view.

Partway up, Adam raised his hand to signal a halt. "This is about the spot I left my horse and went ahead on foot. We should have someone scout ahead to see if they're still in their camp."

"I can do that." Beaver Tail spoke up. "I know the trail."

Frustration churned in Meksem's chest. She hated staying back, but he was right. He did know the trail these Blackfoot dogs would likely follow.

Yet they would leave tracks. Anyone could follow a trail of prints. *She* could follow a trail of prints.

But if something went wrong and the captors realized they were being followed, Beaver Tail would be more likely to know the place they would lie in wait for that scout.

She pressed her lips in a tight line to keep from speaking up. Sometimes silence took more strength than raising one's voice.

"I'll ride with you to where they camped." Adam spoke to his friend, then turned and addressed their group at large. "Once we know for sure they're gone, I'll signal the rest of you to join me there, and we can gather what details they leave behind."

Watching Adam and Beaver Tail ride into the tree cover and make their way farther up the slope tested her self-control. Underneath her, Apash shifted sideways. Meksem forced herself to loosen her legs around the horse, then reached down and patted the mare's shoulder. *Sorry, girl.*

The horse stopped shifting her feet but bobbed her nose with nervous energy. Meksem made sure she wasn't gripping her reins too tight, then stroked the mare's thick winter hair. The horse could sense the coming battle.

To keep herself from bursting with frustration, Meksem began counting trees as she waited for Adam or Beaver Tail to reappear. When she finished with all the individual trunks she could pick out in the woods, she focused her attention on the rock towers in the distance. The first one stood tallest. If she were to climb it, where would she put each of her hands and feet?

A movement jerked her focus back to the trees as Adam emerged from the shadows. He waved them up with a full arm motion. The war party must be long gone, as they'd suspected.

She gave Apash free rein, and the horse charged up the hill at a half-walk, half-jog—as fast as was safe.

When they neared Adam, he turned and faded into the trees again. She ducked under the branches to follow him. All of them riding through the thick woods sounded like a herd of bison.

From in front of her, Adam pointed to a spot on the ground. "This is where I watched from."

The prints from his feet and hands were clear now that she

looked for them. As well as a long line pressed in the snow where he must have laid flat.

She glanced upward where Beaver Tail sat on his horse in a small clearing. When they all joined him there, it only took a moment to see everything necessary. So many prints, along with a few crumbs of roasted meat.

"This must be where they tied the horses." Caleb spoke from where he'd moved a little farther into the trees. "Lots of hoof-prints here. It's hard to tell how many they have."

Adam's face held a grim line as he lifted his gaze in the direction the tracks led. "I think they caught Tesoro, but I can't be sure. I should have come around here and made certain, in case he's still running by himself."

A new worry needled to her belly. She'd assumed Tesoro's tracks had led Adam here. That the Blackfoot band had captured the horse while he ran free, or maybe they'd stolen him.

"You might've been discovered if you stayed longer and moved around them." Beaver Tail studied Adam. "You said you only saw six men?"

He nodded. "I don't know if the seventh was standing guard or with the horses. Or maybe he left them already. When you catch up with them, will you send me a sign to let me know if you see Tesoro?" From the worry lines marking Adam's face, he probably wanted to ride ahead with Beaver Tail to scout, but two men were much more likely to be seen. They couldn't risk it.

Beaver Tail nodded. "If he is not with them, I'll ride back to you so we can find him."

Adam's relief sank into the air around him. "Thank you."

So much they didn't know, and nothing would be clear until they found this group of kidnappers. Meksem motioned Beaver Tail toward the exiting tracks. "Ride on. We will follow."

They rode half the morning, and Adam had to fight to keep his eyes from drifting shut from lack of sleep the night before.

Meksem didn't seem weary at all. The way she scrutinized the land ahead of them, her gaze scanning in a steady half circle around them, she'd clearly shifted into her warrior mind-set. She rode in the lead, but he kept his mount right behind hers, doing his best to fill the role of her second.

Beaver Tail had ridden back to them after a couple hours on the trail, coming only near enough to signal that he'd seen the war party and they had Tesoro.

The relief that flowed through Adam's veins at knowing the horse wasn't roaming the mountain side warred with a fresh flood of anger at the Blackfoot group. Had one of them crept all the way to their camp and stolen the horse? Maybe they'd only seen the horse walking free and caught him for their own. They would be foolish not to claim such a beautiful animal.

At a spot where the ground grew level enough to allow two horses to walk abreast, he rode his horse alongside Meksem's. "When do you think we should attack them?" But *attack* felt too strong a word. They hadn't discussed how they would get the captives free. Steal them away? That was a question he should definitely ask.

"Maybe when they camp at dark. Need to ask Beaver Tail what lies ahead. Must be before they reach a place where others of their people could come to help." She didn't spare him a glance as she spoke, just kept her narrowed gaze scrutinizing the land around them.

Made sense. "Are we going to try to sneak the women and boy out of their camp?"

The lines in Meksem's jaw shifted as she paused, then finally spoke. "I don't know."

Those must have been hard words for her to say. This woman who worked so hard to prove herself capable. But the fact that she would admit her indecision showed wisdom. "We can see the situation, decide what's best." He could only pray they would have time to make a calculated decision. But he knew as well as she did that, if they came upon the right opportunity, they would need to be ready to act. *Be with us, Lord. Guide this mission as You would have us finish it.*

Sometime just before the sun reached the peak of noon, Beaver Tail appeared in the distance, riding toward them at a jog.

When he reached them, Susanna rode to the head of their group to meet her husband. She reached his side and handed him a chunk of camas bread, and a conversation seemed to pass between their gazes.

Adam couldn't help glancing sideways at Meksem. Would that one day be the two of them? He had no misguided notion that she would be the nurturing wife, handing him camas bread before he went off to the hunt.

Even imagining that picture raised the corners of his mouth in a grin, despite the tension swirling inside him. He and Meksem would be partners, each of them bringing their own skills and working together on whatever quest they undertook.

Every part of him wanted that life.

When Meksem's mare gave a restless stomp, Beaver Tail turned from his wife and swept his gaze over them all.

"They are not far ahead. Seven warriors. Women ride tied on their horses. The boy rides with one of the women." He directed that last bit toward Yaka.

"With my woman." The man pushed his horse forward, crowding them. "They are not hurt?"

"I saw no injuries, but I did not get close."

Adam glanced at Meksem to see if the assurance gave her any relief. Her mouth still pinched in a grim line. Was she thinking that since Telípe was with child, much of her possible injury wouldn't be obvious?

He turned back to Beaver Tail. "When do you think would be the best time to approach them?" *Approach* was a much better word than *attack*.

Beaver looked to Meksem, pausing as though hesitant to speak before she gave instructions. "We could try to surprise them when they stop next. But the land is more open around here, so we can't get close without them seeing. I think it better to wait until they camp in darkness. That way they won't have horses already prepared to mount so they can fight back."

Meksem nodded. "A wise plan."

Beaver Tail raised his brows at her. "Do you want to take over scouting?"

She straightened as he spoke and nudged her horse forward before he finished his words.

~

"Four is too many."

Adam could feel the frustration rising from Meksem as she bit out the terse whisper. Darkness had fallen, and they'd made sure to stop well out of hearing range of the Blackfoot group, just in case one of their horses whinnied or made some other loud noise.

But now they were debating who should ride ahead to develop their plan to retake the captives.

"Beaver Tail should go with me because he may know the people," Meksem said. "He can understand what they say. We can only chance one other person at the most." She swung her gaze between Adam and Alahmoot, then translated her words into Salish.

Adam couldn't let her fierceness wear him down. Scouting on horseback in daylight was one thing, but he wasn't about to let Meksem sneak right up to the war party in the dark without him there to watch her back.

But before he could say anything, the Salish brave turned his head and spat on the ground. He loosed a string of words, then paused with his jaw jutted in a fierce pose.

Meksem nodded at the man, then turned to Adam. "He says he's not willing to fight with us about it. He'll stay here with the others."

Adam slid a glance toward the man. Wise words he wouldn't have expected from him. *If* that was exactly what the fellow had said. He slid a look back to Meksem. No twitch of her mouth or twinkle in her eye that would show she'd adjusted the translation.

With weapons at the ready, he crept forward between Meksem and Beaver Tail, staying low and moving fast over the mostly open ground.

A sliver of moonlight pushed through the clouds, shining off the expanse of snow to lighten the night. Not very helpful to hide them.

When they drew near enough to hear a man's voice ahead, they slowed, taking more time to find cover between each forward push. They were only twenty steps or so from the cluster of boulders that hid the camp. The stones formed something of a rock wall, with a few smaller groupings in front. Maybe the boulders would provide cover so they could get a good look at the group without being seen.

Meksem motioned for him and Beaver to stay where they were. He dipped his chin in understanding, but his belly knotted all the way up to his throat as she darted forward to duck behind the first of the rock groupings.

No sounds drifted from the camp. If the enemy saw her, would they call out? Probably not. A well-aimed arrow could put a quick end to her.

Panic welled inside, but he forced himself to take slow

breaths as he scanned each cranny of the rocks. He kept his rifle tucked in the crook of his shoulder so he could aim and fire at the first sign of an enemy.

Meksem became a shadow, shifting to the next stone, fading into the darkness. He no longer had to worry about breathing, as the effort distracted from his focus. Every part of him strained to see what was happening among the shadows of those rocks.

At last, she moved back toward them, enough that he could make out her form, her arms motioning him and Beaver forward. Adam glanced to make sure the man beside him had also seen the command. At Beaver's nod, Adam prepared himself to dart soundlessly the way Meksem had.

He didn't accomplish her stealth, but at least he reached the first set of rocks without making too much noise. He barely dared breathe, although his chest craved to suck in deep gulps of air.

Meksem advanced all the way into the rocky section, crouching just behind the wall of boulders. If she rose up to peer over the top, she would probably see the entire camp. She didn't look back at him, but he had no doubt she knew exactly where he was. Probably followed him with that extra set of eyes positioned in the back of her head.

He eased forward to the next cluster of rocks, but when his foot knocked a loose stone with a clatter, he froze. Perched on his toes, he didn't dare twitch, much less shift to a more comfortable position.

Every part of him strained for noise from the camp ahead.

No sounds came, but something didn't feel right. Maybe his pounding chest was affecting his senses. But outside of his body, the air hung too still.

Then a tiny noise. A gasp?

He raised his rifle into firing position, scanning the rocks for the best place to sight. Would the Blackfoot look over the top of the stones? Or come around one of the sides? Beaver Tail surely had his own gun aimed, and Meksem held her bow at the ready.

The longer the silence held, the tighter Adam's spirit compressed. Should he move closer? The next boulder was larger than the one he knelt behind now. In truth, the stones hiding him only covered half of his crouched form.

Just when he was preparing to shift forward, a scream curdled the air.

Adam dropped sideways out of instinct and barely missed the whizzing sound by his left ear. A head rose above the top of the stone wall, just over the spot where Meksem crouched.

Adam aimed and squeezed his trigger without giving himself time to think about the fact that his bullet might end the man's life.

The head disappeared as crumbs of rock sprayed from the place. Had he hit the stranger? Or did the fellow only duck out of sight?

Meksem was already moving, sprinting down the length of the rock wall as he rammed a new bullet and powder down the barrel of his gun. A blast sounded from behind him, and a man's shout drifted from the camp ahead.

A woman cried out, whether from pain or fear he couldn't tell.

Determination sluiced through him as he set the rear trigger on his rifle and raised the gun to aim again.

Meksem had reached the end of the last of the boulders on the left side and was leaning around them. Within the space of a heartbeat, she reached for an arrow, fit it in the bowstring, and loosed the weapon.

So far, no gunshots had sounded from the Blackfoot, so maybe they didn't have guns—only bows and arrows, knives, hatchets, and a host of other deadly weapons.

Another head rose above the rocks, but before Adam could aim and fire, the man dropped back out of sight. Checking their positions probably.

The woman's cry sounded again, or maybe that of a child. Adam's heart pounded harder. They had to stop this before the captives were hurt.

Seven men against the three of them—they'd never make it by swarming the camp. They'd have to pick the enemy off one at a time while hiding behind the rocks. Maybe Alahmoot and the others would come now that shots had been fired.

Adam gathered himself, then sprinted forward, stopping just beside the place where Meksem had crouched. He kept an eye on the spot where both heads had popped up from the other side.

A flurry of voices sounded from beyond the rocks, and Adam stood enough so he could almost peer over the top. In a quick movement, he raised his head to see over the stone, bringing his rifle barrel with him.

His mind took a moment to make sense of the bodies scrambling on the other side. That huddle of buckskins must be the captives. A warrior stood just behind them with his bow drawn, arrow pointed at Adam.

Aiming his rifle took hours, and Adam braced for the pain of an arrow piercing his forehead even as he squinted and pulled his trigger.

He dropped out of sight before he could see if his bullet found its mark. As he reloaded, he sent a glance sideways toward Meksem.

She no longer hid behind the rocks but had stepped out, a

hatchet poised—or maybe a knife—and struggled in hand-to-hand combat with someone he couldn't see.

His heart lurched to his throat. Grabbing up his half-loaded gun, he lunged that direction. Her petite body would be no match for a strong warrior, no matter how savvy she was. He had to help her.

He'd only rammed the bullet and powder halfway down the barrel of his gun, but now did his best to finish the job while he ran. He didn't have time to withdraw the ramrod before he reached the grappling pair.

The man had bent Meksem backwards, one hand grasping the wrist holding her tomahawk, the other clutching her throat in an awkward grip.

Adam didn't stop to think, just rammed the butt of his gun into the man's face.

With a hard grunt, the fellow loosed his hold on Meksem and crumpled backward.

Adam turned to check on Meksem, but another brave rose up where the first one had fallen, this time aiming his own hatchet at Adam.

He barely had time to lift his gun and absorb the blow with the metal part of his barrel.

The hatchet bounced off with a sharp *clang*, but the warrior kept coming. He thrust his fists toward Adam, one of them slugging him hard in the throat.

His body convulsed with pain, and his mind fought for air even as he twisted to roll the man off him. They both hit the ground hard, landing on their sides.

The warrior sprang up and kicked out. His foot would have thrust hard into Adam's belly, but Adam got his hands up in time to grip the moccasin foot and still the forward momentum. Using that same effort, he thrust the man backward.

Just as the brave was struggling to keep himself from landing on his back again, another body came at them from the right, ramming into the man's side. Sending him sprawling.

Meksem.

Another Indian dove on top of her, a flash of metal gleaming in the moonlight from the knife in his hand.

Adam had no time to gather himself and spring, so he rolled forward, barreling into the man's legs. Something sharp pierced his back, but he pushed as hard and long as he could until he and the brave with the knife tumbled past Meksem.

Adam still clutched his gun in his hands, and he struggled to get his feet underneath him to shove the barrel higher up on the fellow's body. Anything to slow down his assault.

The brave gathered himself at the same time. Adam plunged the butt of his rifle against the knife, knocking the blade from the man's hand. He shoved the gun again into the man's belly, doubling him over. With a well-planted kick, the brave dropped to the ground.

Not dead, just hurting. Hopefully enough to buy them some time.

He spun for the next attacker, but no one leapt at him. Around him, the camp had descended into chaos.

The Salish braves had indeed come to help, and Alahmoot pinned one of the Blackfoot men to the ground. Yaka and Ukugnut together were fending off another.

Caleb knelt beside the captives, and French stood beside them with his gun raised like a club, ready to fend off anyone who dare hurt the women and child.

Beaver Tail crouched over a man lying on his back, blood gushing from his nose. Maybe the brave Adam had struck in the face with the butt of his rifle. The sight of so much blood would turn his stomach if he let himself look overlong. Especially knowing he'd been the one to cause the flow, bringing on the pain that twisted the man's face. He had to remind himself what these strangers were intending to do with the women and child.

He forced his gaze to move on, seeking Meksem. Two men lay on the ground, both with arrows protruding. Adam blinked away from the glazed look in one brave's empty eyes. *God, help his spirit.*

With the man beside him still curled on the ground moaning, there was only one Blackfoot missing.

And Meksem. Where had she gone?

He scanned the group one more time, his gaze lingering on the women huddled near the place he'd first seen them. No sign of Meksem or the missing Blackfoot.

For that matter…

He scanned the women once more. He'd counted three heads and thought the child would be hidden in the center of the huddle. But one of the faces showed the elfin appearance of a young boy.

One of the women was missing.

Purpose surged through Adam. He had to find those three.

Alahmoot turned from the brave he'd been standing over, and Adam motioned him nearer, then pointed to the one huddled beside him. "Tie him." He crossed his wrists in front of him to illustrate his words.

The man strode over, but Adam didn't wait to see if he would follow orders. God would have to sort out the living and the dead. Just now Adam had to find Meksem and help her.

Had the missing warrior tried to steal off with one of the captives? Maybe Meksem had seen and gone after them.

He reached the group of women and child in two long strides, then crouched before them. "Meksem." He made what he hoped was the sign to ask where she went. At least they would know her name. Hopefully.

The youngest woman, the one not much older than a girl, pointed to his right toward a patch of trees in the distance. She didn't speak, and he didn't wait to ask more questions.

As he sprinted that direction, his mind barely registered the tracks marking the snow. With the moonlight illuminating the white landscape, he could see where they entered the trees ahead of him. He pushed harder to close the distance to the woods.

Maybe he should slow to finish loading his gun, but a glance at the weapon as he ran showed the ramrod had fallen out. *No.* Now there would be no way to shoot the gun until after this ruckus ended.

The trees forced him to slow, the canopy above adding extra darkness to the night. He used the reduced pace to listen for sounds around him, but the only noises drifted from the camp behind him. The tracks continued straight through the woods. Had they headed toward horses?

Tesoro.

Where had the Blackfoot hidden their horses? It seemed odd they would tie them so far from their camp.

The ground dipped into a gully that might be a creek, and he followed the footprints through and up the other embankment.

His air came in gasps, but he poured on more speed as he wove through the trees.

Light shone through the woods ahead. Maybe from a clearing?

He forced his pumping legs to slow just before he broke through the edge of trees. Better to know what he was running into.

Horses milled in a small cluster on the left, the white of Tesoro's coat shining in the moonlight on one side of the group. A thread of relief slipped through him, but he turned his attention to scan the rest of the clearing for people.

For Meksem.

His gaze landed on two figures, and his blood stilled in his veins. Meksem crouched in a pose to attack, knife raised in her fisted hand.

Two short strides away from her, a Blackfoot warrior stood

poised with a hatchet in his grip. His free arm was spread wide, expanding his broad shoulders and massive frame. The man had to be as tall and broad as Caleb.

Barely able to be seen behind him, another pair of legs showed, this one clad in buckskin with the fringe of a knee-length dress just visible.

Telípe.

The man's body completely shielded the young woman, proclaiming without words that Meksem would have to go through him to reach her sister. And the brave stood at least a forearm taller than Meksem, maybe more. Opposite him, Meksem looked like of feisty barn cat squaring off with a mountain lion.

Dear Lord, help her. Let me get there in time.

He sprinted forward, gripping his rifle with both hands. If only he'd had time to load the bullet before. He would never cover the twenty strides to reach the dueling pair before the brave struck with his raised tomahawk.

Stop him, Lord. A lightning strike would do the job well.

Meksem crouched even lower, then sprang forward, knife thrust in front of her. She had nothing to protect her from the blow of that tomahawk the warrior would surely crash down on her head.

CHAPTER 22

"No!" Adam screamed the word, using precious breath to stop the scene in front of him while he ran.

The images slowed as the warrior pulled his leg back, twisting to the side away from Meksem's blade. Starting the arc of his arm to slice down on her shoulder.

But then the scene changed, contorting into something that shouldn't be happening.

The warrior stepped back. He drew the arm holding his tomahawk against his side. The figure huddled behind him jumped to the side. A young woman who must be Telípe.

She ran forward, but instead of embracing her sister—and escaping her captor—she planted herself in front of the man. Spreading her arms wide, she shielded as much of him as her smaller form could cover.

Adam didn't stop to consider what the odd action meant, just closed the last of the distance between them as Meksem stopped the swing of her knife, stumbling to the side to keep from hurting the woman.

She drew herself back and raised the knife again, this time

positioning it to throw. Earlier on the journey, she'd proved her skill with the blade. But could she throw the knife so the weapon struck only the man's head or the top of his shoulders? Would she dare risk wounding Telípe?

He plunged to a stop beside Meksem. Raising his rifle, he pointed the barrel at the man's head. The Blackfoot didn't need to know the bullet wasn't loaded properly. Lord willing, staring down the barrel of a deadly weapon would make the man release Telípe.

Or rather—he slid a glance to the young woman blocking their access to the enemy—maybe this would convince Telípe to free herself from the man. What in the world possessed her to act as a human shield for the one who'd kidnapped her?

"Telípe." Meksem's voice came out hard, that of a warrior. Yet he could sense the quiver she was trying to cover. She spoke a few words in their tongue.

Telípe thrust her chin up as she shook her head and responded with a sentence or two of her own. Now, Adam could see the resemblance between the two in the fierce determination that strengthened their features. He'd always admired that trait in Meksem, but seeing it mirrored in Telípe bloomed a burst of frustration in his gut.

"What did she say?" He growled the words loudly enough for only Meksem to hear.

At first, it didn't seem she would answer. Her body coiled tighter beside him, maybe preparing to strike again. Should he ask once more?

"She says he is not like the others. She does not want me to hurt him." Meksem must have bit the words through clenched teeth, for he had to strain to make them out.

Adam swung his gaze up to the man's face again. The brave stood without expression. Not anger nor fear nor the fierce tenderness that mixed in Telípe's eyes. Did he understand what the women were saying?

Meksem spoke to her sister again in their tongue, and Adam could hear the combination of command and pleading. The tone only an elder sibling could master. He'd used the same with Joel more than once.

Telípe only backed nearer the brave, spreading her arms wider. She was practically pressing herself against the man now, and he still didn't move.

Beside him, frustration rose off Meksem in waves. She spoke once more to her sister, and this time seemed to be asking a question.

As Telípe answered, her face softened, and her gaze dipped for half a heartbeat to her belly. The cut of her dress didn't show signs of the baby yet, but with the gentleness in her eyes, the child must still live within her. Then she lifted her focus back to Meksem and finished whatever she'd been saying.

Meksem listened to her sister in silence, and he willed her to look at him. The frustration seemed to have ebbed some while her sister spoke. What was Telípe saying? What was Meksem thinking? Without peering into her gaze, he could only guess.

At last, she did look over at him. "She wants us to let him go free. Let him take his dead and injured." Her words held no emotion, but her eyes spoke of worry. He could well understand her concern.

But surely this wounded and haggard party wouldn't chase after them and try to recover the captives. Maybe some of his group could keep an eye on the Blackfoot while the rest of them headed west toward Telípe's home.

The idea settled in his chest, but it tripped over a question that still lingered, one he saw in Meksem's eyes as well. "What did he do to win your sister's loyalty?"

Meksem shook her head once. "She only said he was kind."

Though Adam's curiosity bloomed, he didn't press it. Meksem would likely pull the tale from Telípe later.

They turned back to the brave, and Meksem communicated

her answer to the man. After trying several languages—including English—to see if he understood, she resorted to the signs all the tribes seem to know.

You will leave this place, go back to your people. Take your dead and wounded. Do not come after us. Her hands flew through the gestures in a rhythmic dance.

Adam had to force himself to look away from her slender fingers to see the man's response.

He spoke a word Adam couldn't distinguish as he signed. *I will.*

Meksem's mouth formed a grim line as she stepped to the side and motioned for the Blackfoot to pass.

Adam didn't miss the grateful glance Telípe sent her elder sister. The two probably needed a moment alone. He fell into step behind the brave, holding his rifle at the ready. "I'll take him back and tell the others what we promised."

~

A while later, Meksem paused with the two horses she led, stopping them just before she stepped out of the grove of trees that separated the Blackfoot camp from the horse corral. So much unrest stirred her spirit, perhaps a moment to gather her thoughts would help.

Leaning against a tree, she stared out at the activity around the camp. Only two Blackfoot men stood on their own strength—Chogan, the man Telípe protected, and the one whose bloody face still bore the mark of Adam's rifle. Two men lay on the ground, still alive, and their injuries looked like they would, in time, heal.

Beaver Tail hadn't known any of this group but had heard of the village they came from. He said the place possessed a reputation for many acts of war. Was she right to allow these four men to go free?

A pang pressed her chest. They'd accomplished the mission —to catch up to the war party and free Telípe and the other prisoners.

She should exult in their success. Rejoice in the coup of three Blackfoot dead and the others wounded into submission. In truth, her training told her she should not have allowed any of them to leave with their lives.

But when Telípe had stopped her from attacking Chogan and told her of his kindness, of the way he'd protected her and the others from the men's cruelty, something had shifted inside her.

Nay, even before Telípe took her bold action, something in Meksem's spirit had hesitated to quench life. Had God created these men too? If God had a good path for them to walk, was she taking away their chance to choose?

The snapping of a twig behind her shifted her focus away from the remnants of the camp.

Adam approached, leading Tesoro and the final horse the Blackfoot had stolen from the Salish camp. Just the sight of him brought a smile in her heart. He'd shown much bravery during the battle and hadn't tried to keep her back from her position as leader. Hadn't attempted to get in her way or protect her when she needed all her focus for the task at hand. They'd worked well together, she couldn't deny it.

And yet her heart longed for so much more than to fight alongside him.

The sound of his steps slowed when he reached her, but instead of coming alongside her, he stopped at her back, laying a hand on her waist. His breath brushed the opposite side of her face, then both his hands slid around her belly. His warm presence stood solid behind her, and she leaned back into the warmth of his hold.

As his cheek rested against her temple, she relaxed against

him, letting him cradle her. This rightness she couldn't deny either.

The warmth of his touch, the steadiness of his love. No matter how quick or impatient his other actions, his love stayed steady. Her heart had never connected with another person's the way it melded with this man's. A breath seeped out of her, but she didn't realize how loud it sounded until his chuckle reverberated against her back.

She didn't try to explain what she was feeling, and she didn't have to. The gentle squeeze of his arms showed he understood.

After a moment, his voice rumbled in her ear. "You seemed deep in thought when I walked up."

How did this man know her so well? She shifted her head sideways to send him a half grin. "You seem to know my mind without me speaking it. You must know what I was thinking." And, if he had any answers for her questions, she would love to hear them.

A grin tipped the corner of his mouth. "I can't read your thoughts unless I can see your eyes. You'll have to tell me this time."

More warmth seeped through her and she settled her head back in the crook of his neck, nestling deeper in his arms. "You look inside me with those special eyes of yours." She kept the words light, even as her mind spun with how to explain what she'd been pondering. Maybe best to start with the choice she'd made. "I have chosen the good path God has for me."

He stilled behind her, and the turning of his mind sounded loud in the midst of his silence. "Just now?" He didn't seem to be breathing. Did this decision mean that much to him?

"Last night, when we were looking for you."

His breath slipped out in a long, slow push, and his body came to life around her. "I'm glad, Meksem." He pressed a kiss to the side of her head and squeezed her waist in a hug. "So glad."

She couldn't help the smile that rose inside her. For a long moment, she let herself sink into Adam's joy.

But as the silence wrapped around them again, she searched for words to finish her thought. "I don't understand what God wants of me. When I stood with my knife poised to end a man's life, something inside me hesitated. As though I was taking away his chance to choose God's good path." She shifted her head sideways again to look at him. "How do I know what God wants of me? Will He tell me?"

There. That was the question she'd been struggling to form in her mind.

Adam's mouth curved again, but this time the smile held a pensive look. "He will. He has. In the Bible He gave us, He tells us how to follow His good path. I wish I still had my Bible, but I left it in Andalusia." Then, his voice turned thoughtful. "I wonder if Beaver or Susanna have one. Mayhap, we can learn His words together."

Hope slipped into her chest. She'd heard of the white man's Bible but hadn't realized the book contained directions straight from God Himself. This way she could learn about the One she'd committed her life to. And learning alongside this man who held her heart would be an adventure all its own.

One every part of her craved to begin.

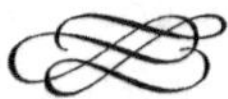

CHAPTER 23

*A*dam settled into the easy rocking of his horse's gait as they maneuvered down the slope in the rear of the long line of riders. These western mountains could barely be called hills compared to the steep cliffs they'd climbed near the center of the range.

The journey back seemed to take half the time compared to the tension-filled trip east, even though they'd allowed themselves to sleep each night through. A lightness had settled over the group, despite the weariness that showed on all their faces and in the slope of their shoulders.

Finally, after almost ten days trekking westward, this would be their last day before reaching the foothills. Then a day over the plains, and they'd arrive at Telípe's village. Actually, most of the people now in their group had come from that Salish camp, but the place stood in his mind as Telípe's home.

He was even enjoying getting to know Meksem's half-sister. The woman didn't speak English, so he could only communicate through Meksem or with his stilted sign language. And though Telípe's winsome features made her seem so young, something about the sadness in her eyes made him think much lay beneath her girlish surface.

He'd not realized until two days ago that Telípe's town was the place where Meksem had lived her first five years. Probably the happiest years of her life, thriving under the care of both her mother and the father she still missed.

He couldn't bring her father back to life, but he planned to do everything in his power to bring back the pleasure she'd enjoyed in those early days. To make her feel loved beyond measure.

Which brought him to the idea that had been circling in his mind through most of the day. The easier return journey had allowed him and Meksem more time together. And when Susanna offered her Bible for him to read, he and Meksem had spent some of his favorite moments talking through passages. The fresh perspective she shared opened his eyes in ways he'd never imagined.

She'd even asked if he'd teach her to read English so she could study the Scriptures herself. As wonderful as the chance for more time together during their lessons sounded, his chest twinged at the thought of not being part of her discovery as she uncovered new truths in the Bible. Not seeing the light of understanding shimmer in her eyes as the Lord's words unfolded to her.

Like every good Spanish boy, he'd been forced to attend services most of his life, but watching her come to life in her hunger for Scripture drew out that same craving in him. He would teach her to read as she asked—and enjoy every minute of her nearness—but then he'd have to be intentional about making sure they studied the Bible together.

And the passage in the Gospel of Mark he'd discovered that morning would be the perfect section to read next. If he could just get her alone, those verses would be an ideal way to ask her the question burning inside him.

He no longer had a doubt Meksem was the one God intended for him, and the time had come to tell her so. The longing and unrest that had plagued him all his life seemed to settle more each day. With this new faith growing inside him—a yearning that Meksem shared just as strongly—his life had never felt so right.

Not that he had any special desire to settle down and sit around a campfire all day like an old man, casting aside all hope for adventure. But he had a feeling life with Meksem would never lack excitement.

He could only pray she longed for that future together as much as he did.

At the base of the mountain they'd been descending, Alahmoot halted them at a patch of trees that stretched the length of the valley. He spoke a string of words in his language, then Meksem turned to translate for the rest of them.

"This is a good place to camp. A river runs through the trees, and the snow is shallow enough the horses can dig for grass."

Adam sat a bit straighter, glancing over the area. With dusk not quite settled, this was earlier than they usually stopped to camp. Surely there would be a quiet spot around here where he could take Meksem to ask his question.

Setting up camp seemed to take forever, and when Meksem volunteered to help gather firewood, he wanted to grab her hand and haul her away. Instead, he finished his work with the horses and joined her to gather his own load.

After they dumped their logs by the growing stack, he turned and gave her a look that brooked no opposition. "I want to show you something."

He should have known better than to have that bit of command in his tone, for she raised her brows and pinched her lips. Would she refuse him? He forced himself to ease his expression into a smile. "Please. I've been waiting all day."

Her teeth slipped over her lower lip as the corners of her

mouth twitched. When her eyes danced like that and she tried to fight a grin, it took everything in him not to pull her into his arms and nibble those lips himself.

At last, she nodded. He turned to his pack and grabbed the leather wrapping that secured the Bible, then started for the trees. "Let's see if we can find someplace quiet."

"Adam."

He paused and glanced back to her. "What's wrong?"

Meksem stood where he'd left her, that untamed expression on her face that he couldn't help but love. "I know of a place. I can show you."

A grin started somewhere in his chest. "Lead the way."

She took him along the edge of the trees, then turned back up the mountain. Boulders and overgrown shrubs soon hid them from camp and the makeshift horse corral.

This place would work. They could easily perch on some of these rocks, or even sit in the snow for all he cared. The location wasn't nearly as important as what he planned to say.

And her answer mattered most of all.

As she climbed up onto a ledge, she glanced back at him with an impish grin. Maybe listening in on his thoughts. "This is it."

"We didn't have to go so far." He pulled himself up beside her. As he straightened and took in the view around him, the soft reverence that had filled her tone seeped into his own chest.

On one side of the ledge lay the valley they'd just hiked through. But on the other...a vast plain stretched before them, sloping hills as far as he could see. The western sky lit with oranges and pinks and purples, the perfect backdrop for what would come next.

Meksem's hand slipped into his, weaving her fingers between his own. He breathed in a deep draught of fresh air, filling his chest with the refreshing goodness.

"I've come here a few times while hunting, and this view speaks to me." She pressed a hand to her chest.

"I know what you mean." That part of his own body ached, and not just from the icy air he inhaled.

She looked over at him. "You wanted to show me something?" Her eyes danced in that way that seemed new these past days. The way that made his heart surge.

Pulling out the Bible, he unwrapped the piece of leather protecting the book. The fluttering in his belly had nothing to do with the cold, nor did the way his hands had begun to sweat. "I found some verses I like. Can I read them to you?"

She nodded, her mouth pulling in an expectant look. Almost like a young girl waiting for a promised sweet.

His fingers fumbled with the pages, but he finally found the verses in the book of Mark, chapter ten. "This is Jesus answering questions from the religious leaders, kind of like the village shaman, and His words speak of something I've been thinking of a lot lately." His mouth tugged in a grin. The moment had come.

He focused in on the black text. "But from the beginning of creation God made them male and female. For this cause shall a man leave his father and mother, and cleave to his wife. And they twain shall be one flesh: so then they are no more twain, but one flesh. What therefore God hath joined together, let not man put asunder." His heart surged at the final words—words often spoken during a wedding.

He raised his gaze to Meksem, meeting her beautiful eyes. "From the moment I met you, something inside me came to life. Like I'd found what I'd been searching for all these years." He lifted the Bible. "These words speak of marriage. Of joining lives. Of joining hearts."

He wanted to put the Bible down and take her hands in his. But her gaze had turned to something he couldn't read. What was she thinking?

Pushing through the fear that suddenly gripped his chest, he forced out the last of what he needed to say. "My heart is yours.

You've won it with your kindness, your bravery, your inner strength. In truth, it would take me all night to list everything I love about you. But now I ask, will you join your heart to mine? Your life with mine? Will you agree to spend the rest of our lives together as man and wife?"

His lungs wouldn't draw breath as he watched her face, studying for what her answer might be.

When her gaze turned glassy, he had to look twice. Tears? From this strong woman? Not at all what he'd expected.

Then her lips pulled into a trembling smile, even as the moisture thickened in her eyes. She nodded, sniffing. "Yes."

A surge of joy spread through him as he closed the Bible and laid it atop the leather strip. Then he reached for her.

She came to him willingly, slipping into his arms where she fit so perfectly. He wrapped her tightly, soaking in the wonder of what was happening. She'd said yes. This remarkable woman had agreed to marry him.

Lord, You're so good to me. She was far beyond what he deserved, but he'd treasure every minute with her.

And all the adventures that lay ahead.

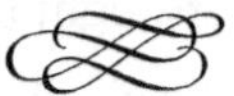

*A*dam's gut clenched as the village of lodges and longhouses spread out before them. He'd not realized the town where Meksem and Elan lived was so large. But then, they'd approached from a different direction last time, back when they'd first headed out to find the war party that had captured Telípe.

He slid a sideways glance at the woman riding tall beside him. Did she regret leaving her sister at the Salish camp that morning? Telípe and the other Salish captives and rescuers had been welcomed with feasting, yet Meksem had held herself a little distant from the celebrating. She hadn't seemed comfortable, yet he couldn't tell whether her discomfort came from so many strangers...or maybe from the village itself. A few times she'd scanned the lodges with pain furrowing her brow. Did she have memories of her father in that place? If so, did the town look different than she remembered? Surely the place would have changed after so many years.

He wanted to ask, but she would tell him when she was ready. There had simply been too many people around, never allowing them a moment alone. Maybe she'd speak her thoughts once they were settled in her town, snuggled beside a lodge fire. Even now, sitting atop horses with their friends surrounding them, his arms ached to hold her.

Soon, she would be his in every way, just as God intended. They'd already talked to Caleb about performing a marriage service. Meksem said the Nimiipuu ceremony was more of a feast with a gift exchange, so it should be easy to combine the Christian traditions with that of her people. They could do the official exchange of vows before God, then celebrate with food and gifts—not unlike the weddings his parents forced him and Joel to attend back in Andalusia.

Except this time he was actually looking forward to the event. Could hardly wait for the day.

But first, he had to obtain his gift for her.

His mouth went dry at the thought. Caleb and French had offered to ride with him to the Kannah village where Meksem had traded her family heirloom. They'd spend a few days in this town first. Joel would surely be married now, and probably wouldn't want to set out on another journey so soon, even a short one.

A familiar pang pressed in his chest. He'd always regret missing Joel's wedding. There hadn't seemed to be a way around it—he'd needed to help Meksem and it would have been selfish to ask Joel and Elan to wait. Still…

"There is Elan." Meksem's voice drew him from his thoughts, and he squinted into the distance.

Two forms strode toward them from the camp, and one possessed the determined manner so familiar. A smile pushed out from the fullness in his chest. "Joel, too." He'd never been so happy to see his little brother marching toward him.

Minutes later, he slid from his mount and reached for Joel's outstretched hand, pulling him into a hug.

"It's about time." Joel's voice graveled as Adam held him a second longer than necessary.

Breathing in Joel's familiar scent, gripping solid muscle that had been weak when he left his brother a month before—he'd not realized how much he'd been worried about Joel's recovery. How much he'd missed him.

Stepping back, Adam ran his gaze over his brother's face, then down the length of him. "You're looking a great deal better than when we left." His skin had regained a healthy tan, and life glimmered in his eyes again.

Then Adam couldn't help shifting his focus to the woman standing a little back from them, with Meksem by her side, both of them watching him and Joel. He gave Elan a nod of greeting, even as his gut tightened. "Hello, Elan. Do I say welcome to the family yet?" He slid a look back to Joel for confirmation.

His brother's face took on the closest thing to a silly grin he'd worn since he was ten years old. He turned and drew Elan up beside him. "Not yet." Then he gave Adam a meaningful look. "We're awful glad you're back. Wasn't sure how much longer we'd have to wait."

Adam struggled to make sense of the words. "But...I told you not to hold the wedding for me. Were you waiting for Caleb?" That made more sense. Joel might also want his ceremony performed by a minister ordained of God.

He raised his brows. "Him, too. But I couldn't imagine having an important event like that without you here. Nothing about it felt right."

Pleasure spread through Adam like a warm drink on a cold night. He let his grin show. "Sorry to keep you waiting then."

He couldn't help a glance at Meksem. She met his gaze, her own joy shining in her eyes. She didn't speak often of her friendship with Elan, but the two seemed to hold a bond almost as strong as sisters.

He turned back to Joel and Elan, even while he moved to Meksem's side and slipped an arm around her. "Good. You can set the date for any day now." Then he turned and started them toward the village. "I hope you have a warm fire here. I don't think my toes have thawed in a month."

As Joel fell into step beside him, Adam didn't release his arm from around Meksem. The weight of his brother's gaze heated the side of Adam's face, and he shot a grin sideways. Joel was surely wondering about what had happened between the two of them on the journey.

But surprise wasn't the expression marking his features. Nope. A smirk tipped Joel's lips—the kind that said he'd expected this completely. Adam barely kept himself from cuffing the fellow on the arm. Some little brothers would always be impertinent.

But he settled for a shameless grin. Impertinent or not, he couldn't deny how glad he was to see Joel's face.

~

*M*eksem strained to make out the English words Caleb spoke over Elan and Joel. Even though some of the language made no sense, the beauty of the ceremony swelled a lump in her throat. The way he spoke God's name over each part, asking Him to unite the couple and bless their lives together, opened her mind to a host of new ideas. Could a marriage be holy?

She slid a glance at Adam, standing beside his brother. He was already looking at her, and his eyes pulled her in just like they always did. *I want our marriage to be holy.* Could he hear her thoughts?

The idea started a longing in her spirit. *Bless us, Lord. Join us together in Your hands.*

The rest of the ceremony passed in a blur, especially since she couldn't take her eyes from the man standing across from her. The man who would be hers soon.

How soon? He wouldn't say when, only that there was one

thing he needed to do first. She had a feeling she knew what that *one thing* might be, and the possibility stirred a different kind of yearning inside her.

The moment Caleb finished the ceremony, Adam stepped to her side. His gaze had turned smoldering, and his nearness took her breath.

"Come with me?" He phrased it like a question, but something in his tone made her fairly certain that if she said no, he'd sweep her into his arms and carry her wherever he planned to go.

The thought flushed heat through her veins. Perhaps she should test him.

But instead, she took his hand and followed as he slipped to the side of the group gathering around Joel and Elan. Maybe she should tell her friend again how happy she was for her. For both friends, since Joel could be claimed by that name, too.

Later. When so many people weren't crowded around them. And when she didn't have such an alluring distraction in the form of the man half-dragging her toward the edge of the village.

When they reached a spot out of sight of most of the others, he turned and pulled her into his arms. She went willingly, raising her face to meet his.

His kiss was full of the same intensity his eyes had held throughout the ceremony, speaking of his love for her. His longing for her. The same that burned inside her.

Yet, she was safe in his kiss. His touch bespoke protection, even from himself.

He drew back with a groan long before she was ready. "Soon, Meksem. Our day will be soon." He slid his hands from her back, his fingers dragging all the way down her arms to cup her hands. His touch lighting her skin on fire, even through her leathers.

After pressing a kiss to the tips of her fingers, his gaze pulled her nearer as his eyes turned earnest. "I need to go back to the Kannah village, the town where you all first found me. Caleb and Joel are coming too. Would you like…?" His voice trailed off, as though he hadn't intended to add the last part.

She'd been right then. Still, she had to ask. "You're going to get my father's tomahawk?"

His mouth formed a reluctant smile. "I'd hoped to surprise you."

She studied him, every perfect feature. Did she dare say what she wanted to? She must. A holy marriage couldn't start off by holding things back. "You won't give up Tesoro?"

The air between them grew thicker as he seemed to be struggling with something, either what his decision would be or what he should say to her. "I'd rather not."

"I don't want you to." She let her determination show in her eyes. His happiness meant more to her than a possession, especially since she still carried with her memories of her father. Memories she'd hold dear for all her days.

"I won't then." He pressed his forehead to hers, and the love in his voice made her heart ache more than she'd ever imagined possible.

The only way she could respond was with the phrase he'd taught her. "*Te amo*, Adam Vargas." She loved these words from his native language. Loved the way they rolled off her tongue. Loved the special light that glowed in his eyes when she said them.

He pressed another kiss to her mouth, this one so achingly gentle every part of her responded. When he pulled back, he rested his head on hers again, but his hands seemed to quiver as they cupped hers. "So what do you think, come with me?" A rasp had slipped into his tone. Maybe he was struggling for control as much as she was.

"You think I'll let you go without me?" Her voice wasn't quite as strong as usual. A bit more breathy. A surprising sound, for being so near this man now stole her breath.

His mouth curved in a grin. "It might be an adventure."

A fresh wave of warmth swept through her. "With you, I would expect nothing less."

Did you enjoy Meksem and Adam's story? I hope so!
Would you take a quick minute to leave a review where you purchased the book?
It doesn't have to be long. Just a sentence or two telling what you liked about the story!

To receive a free book and get updates when new Misty M. Beller books release, go to https://mistymbeller.com/freebook

Chapter One

Early Sring, 1832
Clearwater River Valley, Future Idaho Territory

Even as a grown man, Caleb Jackson still craved the familiar.

And the sight of the familiar Nez Perce camp stretching out ahead of him settled around Caleb like the soft blanket he'd carried far too long through his boyhood years.

It'd been weeks since he and his friends had left this village, and they'd been to two other camps since. But something about this one had seeped into his soul and felt a little more like home. A strange feeling when he didn't even speak their tongue.

Maybe he'd connected with this place because the people here had been so welcoming. His first taste of the Nimiipuu way of life.

It didn't hurt that the maidens here were quite pleasant to

look at. Especially one, in particular, although perhaps she wouldn't be called a maiden. She'd been married once, and from what he'd gathered, her husband had died just before the birth of their son. A cute little chap about two years old who seemed to get into trouble an awful lot for his chubby little legs.

A movement to the right of the camp near the river swung his gaze. Surely that couldn't be the lad he'd just been thinking of, toddling away from the lodges toward the deep currents.

The figure was definitely a child, around the age of River Boy.

Caleb's heart hurtled into his throat, and he spun his horse toward the lad, digging in his heels. The mare sprang into action, surging into canter. He pushed her faster as he bent low over the horse's neck.

Hadn't the lad learned his lesson the last time he played too close to the water's edge? Joel and Adam had barely saved him from freezing to death with his leg caught in the ice that crusted the murky surface. Then Joel had narrowly escaped with his own life when the ice broke through while they crossed back over the river.

Caleb squeezed his legs tighter, urging the mare faster to close the last thirty strides. The lad had only two steps to reach the bank now. Where was the boy's mother? How could he have wondered out of her sight? Again.

With no father to provide for the family, she must be carrying the burden of too much responsibility on her shoulders to keep such an active child contained. A situation he was far too familiar with.

Determination surged through him as the lad splashed into the water, his black head dipping with each step he toddled down the bank.

Caleb locked his eyes on those dark locks and pushed the mare harder. The puff of hair dropped lower when the lad sat in the water. Maybe his feet had been jerked from under him by the swift-flowing current. At least there was no ice now. Was that a good thing? The snow melt from the mountains had filled the river, threatening to burst beyond its banks.

The mare neared the river, and Caleb sat back in the saddle, pulling hard on the reins to slow the horse. He leapt to the ground before she stopped and closed the last strides to the water, even as the boy's dark hair floated away from the bank.

A child's laugh sounded, and the boy splashed in the rushing water, despite the fact it was carrying him far from shore—faster and faster with each heartbeat. Did he not know the swift current held his life in its clutch? The lad knew no fear. Especially not the healthy kind.

Caleb sprinted three long strides along the bank's edge, just enough to get ahead of where the boy floated. Then he launched into the icy water. The cold sucked his breath, clamping hard on his chest with its frigid claws.

Gathering his wits, he mentally scrambled for anything he could recall about the water levels. The stretch nearest the bank dipped quickly to waist level. But with the extra liquid flowing down from the mountains, he had to break into a swim after only one step. Three powerful strokes brought him within reach of the lad.

He grabbed an arm and held tight, planting his feet in front of him and paddling backward to stop the river's grip.

Drawing the boy close to his chest, Caleb swam toward the shore. A group of people had gathered there—his friends, from the quick glance he managed between swimming strokes.

At last, hands reached out to him, one grabbing his arm and the others taking the boy. Still laughing, River Boy kicked his pudgy arms and legs the whole way up.

For Caleb's part, exhaustion weighed his bone-chilled limbs now that fear no longer drove him. He pulled himself up on the bank, crawling to a dry spot to sit.

"Here, Caleb, let's get you out of these wet things." Susanna,

Beaver Tail's wife, crouched in front of him and began unbuttoning his coat. She was right, the furs had taken on water, and maybe its weight was part of what stole his strength.

He took over unfastening the buttons and slipped the heavy coat off. His buckskin tunic underneath was mostly dry, except around the collar, sleeves, and waist.

He glanced up at Susanna with a nod of thanks. "That's better."

Now that he'd caught most of his breath and a little of his energy, he turned to where the boy was being tended to.

His gaze landed on an image that once again stole his breath. The lad's mother ran to her son, and now cradled him in a tight embrace.

Otskai was even more beautiful than his memories of her. Her face clear. Not a wrinkle or blemish to be found. So young. His heart ached. She was too young to already be a widow, raising this son on her own.

Then she lifted her dark lashes and cast her wide gaze toward Caleb. The whites of her eyes glimmered red, so full of unshed tears the pressure in his chest tightened tenfold.

"Thank you." Her words came out in a thick accent, but she spoke English. The first he'd heard from her.

The weight on his chest loosened enough for his heart to ramp into another gallop. What was wrong with him, letting himself fall so hard for a woman he barely knew?

He felt for her predicament. Worried over her son and the boy's penchant for danger. But Caleb had never thought to find anything more. Never had he wanted more from the woman.

He forced his gaze away from hers, letting his focus drop to the boy. The lad curled against his mother, cheek resting on her shoulder with a thumb in his mouth. Perfectly content in the loving protection of her arms.

A burn crept up Caleb's throat. They made such a perfect

picture, this woman and boy. He barely knew them, but the pair had already managed to plant themselves firmly in his thoughts, even when he was an entire mountain range away.

He needed some space. With a flick of his gaze to her eyes, he nodded. "You're welcome." He wanted to know how the boy had wandered away by himself, but he'd have to ask that later.

For now, he grabbed his coat and pushed to standing, then marched toward his mare. He owed the girl a walk to dry her sweaty sides, and a good brushing. Maybe that would give them both enough time to cool off.

Otskai clutched her son to her chest as she watched the big man gather his horse's reins and lead her away. She should stand and take her son back to their lodge, but fear had leaked away all her strength. How many times would this boy scare her lifeless?

So far, these white men had saved River Boy twice. Both times, her son would have died if they hadn't reached him in time. Neither time had she been there. She'd not been what her child needed. The guilt would smother her if she let it, but she couldn't give in to such weakness.

River Boy squirmed in her tight hold, a good reminder that she had to get him back to the lodge and out of his wet clothes. The last thing he needed was a sickness from the remnants of this winter wind.

After pressing a final kiss to his damp hair, she stood and gripped his chubby little hand. The lad tried to dart ahead, but she'd learned to keep a tight hold.

One of the Nimiippu women who'd come with the white men was lingering nearby, and Otskai worked for a smile. "Elan?" She remembered this one, from a village of the Pikunin band to the north. The first time she'd met Elan, she'd been struck by the fact that the meaning of her name matched her personality—friendly.

The woman nodded with a return smile that didn't mask the concern in her eyes. "I see River Boy is still living up to his name."

Otskai sent a wry look toward the rushing water, fighting off the shiver that always coursed through her at the sight of the churning bubbles. "Perhaps if I change his name, he'll change his ways."

Her deceased husband's parents had christened the lad River Boy after his first escapade in the water, back when he could only crawl. He'd been in their care while she worked to get enough baking done for the week. The lad had crawled right to the edge of the bank and tumbled head-over-toes into the water.

She'd been so relieved they pulled him out safely, she'd accepted the new name. Especially since she'd never really liked the one Motsqueh had given him before his birth.

Maybe if she'd fought this new title, her son wouldn't have developed this deadly love of rushing water. It seemed no matter how careful she was, he still found a way to sneak out of her focus and escape to the river.

She turned her focus away from those thoughts and toward the camp, refreshing her grip on her son's hand. "I must get him back and changed."

Elan fell into step on River Boy's other side. "Can I walk with you? Joel has my horse, and I need to find my aunt and uncle to see if we can use their extra lodge while we're here."

Otskai didn't answer the question. She would have preferred to be alone, but she liked this woman. "You are staying long this time?"

Elan shook her head. "My husband's brother has business with your chief. Once that is finished, we'll return to the village of my people." She sent Otskai a grin. "I think. My husband and his brother seem drawn to adventure, so I can't say firmly we'll stick to that plan."

Husband. The last time they'd been here, Otskai well remembered Elan pining over one of the two white men who had been ill. The two who had saved River Boy.

She raised her brows. "You're married now?"

A pretty flush spread across Elan's face, a sign this was a very new event. And it surely was, for it had been less than two moons since they'd left, if she remembered correctly.

Elan dipped her chin in a nod. "To Joel. He is the one who had been shot before." Elan pressed a hand to her belly to show the place the bullet had struck. Then all trace of pleasure left her face. She must have remembered the part Joel played in saving River Boy.

Better to speak of that day openly so it wouldn't hang heavy between them. "He is the one who nearly died saving my son." She met the woman's eyes boldly. "I owe a huge debt to him. And to the other man for his bravery this day. You are all welcome to anything I have. Including space in my lodge."

She hadn't thought ahead to that offer, but it seemed the only decent thing to say. The tiny teepee she and her son shared was barely big enough to hold their supplies, but they could move outside to sleep if they needed to. She couldn't withhold shelter from these people who done what she'd been unable to. Twice now.

Elan's smile was soft. "You owe us nothing, but I thank you for the offer. My aunt's lodge is large and should be more than we need. We would love for you to share a meal with us though. Perhaps tomorrow at sunset?" Elan's gaze probed, seeking out agreement.

Otskai nodded. In truth, she couldn't say no. Yet something inside her said more time spent with these newcomers might disrupt all the hard work she'd put into building her future.

Yet how could it? This was simply a meal, one more time to express gratitude for another selfless act.

Good thing she'd been learning to speak the white man's tongue.

Get COURAGE IN THE MOUNTAIN WILDERNESS at your Favorite Retailer!

ABOUT THE AUTHOR

Misty M. Beller is a *USA Today* bestselling author of romantic mountain stories, set on the 1800s frontier and woven with the truth of God's love.

She was raised on a farm in South Carolina, so her Southern roots run deep. Growing up, her family was close, and they continue to keep that priority today. Her husband and children now add another dimension to her life, keeping her both grounded and crazy.

God has placed a desire in Misty's heart to combine her love for Christian fiction and the simpler ranch life, writing historical novels that display God's abundant love through the twists and turns in the lives of her characters.

Connect with Misty at www.MistyMBeller.com

    1. Hope's Highest Mountain
    2. Love's Mountain Quest
    3. Faith's Mountain Home

Call of the Rockies

    1. Freedom in the Mountain Wind
    2. Hope in the Mountain River
    3. Light in the Mountain Sky
    4. Courage in the Mountain Wilderness